SECOND CHANCES

TERESA ROMAN

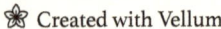 Created with Vellum

DEDICATION

For my children,
who bring me through the darkest moments of life.

1

If tossing and turning were an Olympic sport, I'd be a gold medalist. I seemed to have reached the point where I could no longer fall asleep without the help of pharmaceuticals. Every night was the same. As soon as I got into bed, my brain would fill with the same unrelenting, intrusive thoughts. I reminded myself for the hundredth time that I didn't have the power to turn back time, so there was no point in dwelling on mistakes I couldn't undo.

After an hour I gave up the struggle, got out of bed, and popped a melatonin into my mouth. It took longer to work than I wanted it to, but eventually I drifted off, not waking until the morning.

Instead of the alarm or the sound of the garage door opening as my husband Ryan got home from another graveyard shift at the hospital, it was the phone that pulled me out of my sleep. I glanced at the bedside clock and immediately panicked. Seven thirty. That meant I only had half an hour to dress and get the kids ready for school. I must've slept through the alarm or forgotten to turn it on.

I reached for the phone, hoping that whoever it was they'd

spit out whatever they had to say quickly. "Hello," I said, my voice still heavy with sleep.

"Is Vanessa Collins available?"

"Who's calling?" I asked.

"This is Dr. Mallet. I'm a physician in the emergency room at Sacramento Valley Hospital."

That was the hospital where Ryan worked. "My husband's not home from work yet," I said. "But I can leave a message for him if you like."

It suddenly dawned on me that it was strange Ryan hadn't made it back yet. The hospital wasn't that far. He got off at seven, and it never took him longer than twenty minutes to get home.

"Well, it's not him I need to speak to. It's you," the doctor said, his voice gentle. "I'm calling because your husband was involved in a motor vehicle accident on his way home from work this morning."

For a moment, I couldn't think of what to say. "Is he all right?"

"I'm afraid not, Mrs. Collins. Unfortunately, he was in critical condition when the paramedics brought him in. He went into cardiac arrest in the ambulance on the way to our hospital. We did everything we could for him, but he didn't make it. He passed away a few minutes ago."

"He what?" I asked, feeling like the air had been sucked out of me.

"I'm sorry to have to tell you this, but your husband passed away."

If it weren't for the sound of my kids in the kitchen I would've sworn that I was still asleep and in the midst of some bizarrely realistic dream. "Are you sure it's really him?"

"Yes, ma'am, we're sure."

A sudden wave of dizziness came over me. Thankfully, I was

still in bed, or I would've probably lost my balance and fell to the floor. I was too stunned to think of anything to say.

"Mrs. Collins? Are you still there?"

"Yes, I'm here."

"I expect you'll want to see him before he's taken to the morgue."

"I ... I have to take my kids to school," I said. As those words left my mouth, I wondered if that was right. Their father had just died. Surely that warranted missing a day of school. But I couldn't bring them to the emergency room with me. They were too young. I couldn't picture either of my kids handling the sight of their father's dead body. The last thing I wanted to do was traumatize them. "But I'll come down right after that."

"Okay," Dr. Mallet said. "We'll see you soon. Be sure to ask for me when you come by. I just started my shift, so I'll be here all day." He cleared his throat and continued. "I'm very sorry for your loss."

The doctor hung up, and I just sat there for a minute, trying to process everything. Ryan couldn't be dead. That's why I wasn't crying. Or maybe it was because I knew I couldn't break down in front of the kids. I made a point of never crying in front of them because I was their mom, and mothers needed to be strong for their children. Despite my brain fog, I managed to get out of bed and pull on a pair of yoga pants and a T-shirt. Just then Lydia walked into the bedroom.

"You do know what time it is, right, Mommy?"

"Yes, yes, yes. I know."

Hands on her hips, she said, "I don't want to be late for school."

"You won't be," I replied. "See, I'm already dressed."

Lydia turned around, and I followed her down the hallway and into the kitchen, where my son, Jacob, sat at the table, a bowl of cereal in front of him. "How come Daddy's not home yet?"

I stared at him, tongue-tied for a moment. "He's just running a little late. I'm sure he'll be home soon." Had I just lied to my child? *Ryan's not dead.* This whole thing had to be one huge misunderstanding.

"We have to leave in ten minutes," Jacob said.

I took a deep breath, trying to keep myself from having a full-blown panic attack. "Did you and your sister finish packing your lunches?"

"Yes," Lydia chimed in. "But I haven't had breakfast yet."

"You know how to pour yourself a bowl of cereal," I said.

"I don't want cereal. I'm sick of cereal."

I was about to snap at her but forced myself to stop. I needed to hold it together for my kids' sake. Once I got them to school, I'd be able to sort everything out. A part of me believed that I'd show up at the hospital to find that the doctor who'd called earlier had made a giant mistake. Ryan could not be dead. This day would be like any other. I'd take the kids to school, come back home, scarf down a quick breakfast, and get to work while Ryan slept after coming home from a twelve-hour night shift. Around three, just after returning home from picking our kids up from school, Ryan would amble into the kitchen, grumbling about his coworkers and how much he hated his job, while I did my best to come up with encouraging words.

"I don't have time to make you eggs. How about a piece of toast?"

"Only if you put honey on it."

I smiled at her. Lydia was my sassy child, but I couldn't help but love her spirit. "I wouldn't dare make it any other way."

A FEW MINUTES later the three of us rushed out of the house.

Lydia still had her half-eaten toast in one hand. I dropped them off, giving them each a kiss on the cheek and then watching as they ran into the school building before driving away.

It was only then, after morning drop-off, that the rush of the morning dissipated. With the kids safely in their classrooms I could *really* think about Ryan and the phone call I'd received earlier. I was still sure that Ryan wasn't dead. It had to be a mistake, but if it was, then where the hell was my husband? Ryan was never more than a few minutes late. He was also one of the most careful drivers I knew, so it seemed impossible that he'd gotten into a car accident. I sighed as I drove off. The only way I'd know for certain was to go to the hospital and see for myself.

Morning traffic was a nightmare, which further frayed my nerves. Normally, it took me less than fifteen minutes to get to the hospital where Ryan worked. Instead, it took me nearly half an hour. By the time I arrived, I was wound as tight as a spool of thread. *Ryan cannot be dead. Ryan cannot be dead.* Those words echoed in my head over and over as I headed toward the emergency-room entrance.

Since Ryan had taken a job as an X-ray tech at Sacramento Valley Hospital five years ago, I'd been by to see him a handful of times, so I knew my way around fairly well.

I walked up to the emergency room's registration area.

"Can I help you?" a young woman behind a glass partition asked.

"Um, yeah. I'm here to see Dr. Mallet."

"Your name?"

"Vanessa Collins," I said.

"Just one minute." She took off down the hallway behind her. My heart pounded while I waited. *Ryan cannot be dead. Ryan cannot be dead.*

When she returned it was with an older man at her side. He

opened the door that separated the waiting area from the emergency room and ushered me inside.

"Are you Dr. Mallet?" I asked.

"Yes." He extended his hand, and I shook it. The doctor wore navy-blue scrubs, had salt-and-pepper hair, and a calm disposition that put me just a tiny bit more at ease. "It's a pleasure to meet you, Mrs. Collins. I'm just sorry that it has to be under these circumstances."

I didn't know what to say to that, so I just nodded.

"Are you waiting for more family or friends?" he asked.

I shook my head. "No." There really wasn't anyone to wait for. Ryan's family didn't live in California, and he didn't have any close friends.

I followed Dr. Mallet down the hall, through one more door, and down another hall before turning into one of the patient rooms. The doctor glanced at me before pulling back a curtain to reveal a gurney—with my husband lying on it. I sucked in a breath at the sight of him and then covered my mouth with my hand. That dizzy sensation returned and buckled my knees. Dr. Mallet caught me and helped me over to an empty chair.

My chest tightened, and I struggled to catch a breath. I willed myself to calm down then looked up at the doctor. "How could this have happened?"

"Night shifts are tough. The paramedics think Ryan fell asleep at the wheel. His car was hit head-on. He had a lot of internal bleeding, and by the time he was brought here, it was just too late."

"I ... I can't believe it," I said, my voice barely above a whisper. Of course the doctor hadn't made a mistake. Things like that didn't happen in real life. How could I have thought otherwise? Dr. Mallet wouldn't have called me if he hadn't been sure who Ryan was.

My heart sank. How the hell was I supposed to tell my children their father was dead? The thought of it made me sick to my stomach.

I had the hardest time bringing myself to turn my head and look at Ryan. I'd never seen a dead body before. Save for a few small cuts that must've come from the windshield shattering, his face was undamaged. His skin was drained of color, and his eyes were closed. A sheet was pulled up to just under his chin.

Widows were supposed to cry at the sight of their dead husband's body, but my eyes were dry. I didn't know what to say or do. I felt like I was in a state of suspended animation.

"I should leave you alone," Dr. Mallet said. "We'll talk more whenever you're ready. Just ask one of the nurses to page me."

I wanted to grab his hand and tell him not to leave, but that would be crazy. For a minute, I just sat there trying to sort through my thoughts. It had been a mistake to send the kids to school. I should've kept them home. But I was in a rush and not thinking. Apparently, I was just as bad a mother as I had been a wife. The thought finally sent rivers of tears streaming down my face.

2

I sat there crying for a few minutes. Then somehow, I managed to make it to my feet and took a few steps closer to where my husband lay. How was it possible that he was dead? Ryan was a night owl. He grumbled about his work all the time, but he always said he preferred the night shift.

He barely looked like the man I'd met just a little over ten years ago. My thoughts traveled back to that day. It was in a bookstore of all places, the one in which I worked while I was in college. Ryan had come in looking for a book he needed for school. Gross anatomy. While we searched the shelves, looking for the right book, we got to talking. He was finishing up his last few X-ray technician classes.

"I'm also in my last semester," I'd told him.

"Oh yeah? What are you studying?"

"Human resource management." It sounded so boring compared to his major.

After he was done with his purchase, he came back to ask for my phone number. I tried to play it cool as I wrote it down on the back of a store flyer and handed it to him. I wasn't one to give out my phone number to every guy who asked for it, but Ryan was handsome, and in the few minutes we'd talked, I felt a connection. Something about his personality drew me in.

Ryan was a romantic and not just in the bring-you-flowers-and-pay-for-dinner kind of way. Whenever we went out, he opened doors for me, held my hand as we walked, and insisted on carrying my bags for me. I fell for him fast and hard. Two months into our relationship, he proposed. We'd just had sex when he turned on his side to look at me and said, "I think we should get married."

I didn't respond, figuring it was just one of those things guys sometimes said in the afterglow of a passionate lovemaking session. It was sweet, but I didn't think he was *actually* proposing.

"Well, are you going to answer me or not?"

I furrowed my brows in confusion. "You didn't ask me anything."

"Yes, I did," he insisted. "I just asked you if you wanted to marry me."

I wondered how far he'd take this little game of his. Just for the heck of it, I decided to play along. "No, technically you didn't ask. You just said we should get married."

"Fine. Will you marry me?" he asked, too shy to meet my gaze. "Is that better?"

I sat up and lifted his chin with my hand. Maybe he wasn't playing a game. "You're serious? You really want me to marry you?"

"Yes." He stared back at me with those gorgeous brown eyes of his.

"Do I get a ring?" I wasn't one of those women who'd dreamed of getting the perfect diamond ring, but a proposal didn't seem real without something to wear on my finger.

"I want to buy you something amazing. I just don't have the money right now."

"It doesn't matter," I said, realizing I'd probably just embarrassed him. Ryan was almost done with his X-ray tech training. Until he passed his license exam and got his first job, his income was as measly as mine. "I don't care about rings."

"Well, I do. And once I get enough money, I'm going to buy you a diamond big enough to blind you."

I leaned down to kiss him. I didn't doubt that he'd keep his word. Despite his limited funds, Ryan was generous with gifts. "The answer is yes," I said, ignoring the tiny, soft whisper in the back of my head that told me I was crazy for agreeing to marry someone I'd only been dating for a couple of months. "I'd love to marry you."

He kissed me and pulled me down on top of him, rolling me over until my back was pressed against the bed. I felt him grow hard and spread my legs in anticipation. Ryan had amazing stamina when it came to sex. He could get hard again minutes after climaxing. On the nights we spent together at my place or his, I barely slept because he was up every few hours whispering into my ear that he wanted me. And I never minded. He made me feel beautiful, desirable. It hadn't taken long for me to fall madly in love with him. I wanted to make him happy. I wanted to be perfect for him.

Looking back, it was hard to say exactly when things between Ryan and me started to fall apart. It was probably before he slid an elegant pear-shaped diamond ring on my finger, the one he'd promised to get me, and definitely before we exchanged our vows. But love had blinded me. I refused to listen to my friends who told me I was crazy for jumping into marriage so quickly.

I choked back more tears as I thought about the misery Ryan and I had fallen into. For years—I wasn't even sure how many—neither of us had been happy. Half the time, I hated his guts.

And now he was dead. I didn't know what to feel. Regret, relief, guilt, fear, sadness, a mixture of all those things?

What was I going to tell the kids when they got home from school? I had no idea how I was going to get the words out. Between the mountain of unhappy memories I had of Ryan, and the complete shock of his death, not to mention the daunting prospect of single motherhood, I wasn't sure I had anything left to spare. How was I supposed to comfort my children when I felt like I was on the verge of falling apart?

I pushed away the panic that gripped my heart. *Pull yourself together.* I was a grown woman, a mom. I could handle this. Over the past few years, I'd contemplated asking Ryan for a divorce at least half a dozen times. But then I'd imagine life as a single mother and feel overwhelmed. Now, I had no choice. Was this karma biting me in the butt? It didn't matter. I'd find a way to be the best single mother on the planet. I had a shitty childhood. When my kids were born, I vowed to do everything in my power to give them the kind of life I'd dreamed about as a kid. Ryan or no Ryan, I wasn't about to break that promise.

I took a deep breath and brushed my hand on Ryan's shoulder. The sheet kept me from actually touching his skin. It creeped me out to think of what it would feel like. I'd never liked hospitals and left the room whenever Ryan turned on one of his favorite medical dramas or hospital reality shows. He liked talking about his gory patients, people with broken bones poking through open flesh or who'd accidentally chopped off a fingertip with a skill saw. His stories turned my stomach, and I tuned him out whenever he shared one of them, even though he'd get angry whenever he thought I wasn't paying attention to him. It was one of the seemingly thousand things that caused friction in our marriage.

I stared down at the man that had been my husband for the past ten years and whispered, "I'm so sorry. For everything."

Then I turned around and walked out of the room.

A nurse ushered me to a private seating area where I waited for Dr. Mallet. He walked over to me a few minutes later and took a seat in a chair across from me.

"Are you all right?" he asked.

"I'm still so shocked," I replied. "I just never expected something like this would happen."

"It's a shock to all of us." The doctor shook his head. "Ryan was a good man."

I wondered how well he actually knew Ryan, and then I wondered if he actually meant those words or was just saying them because that's what was expected when someone died. Ryan almost never had anything good to say about any of the people he worked with, but I hadn't remembered him mentioning Dr. Mallet's name in the past, so perhaps the two of them had a good working relationship. Or maybe their paths hadn't crossed all that often. I had no idea how often an emergency room doctor and an X-ray tech actually interacted.

"So what happens next?" I asked. "Will he get an autopsy?"

"Ryan died in the hospital, and we know the cause of his death. Under those circumstances, an autopsy usually isn't done. Unless of course you request one."

I shook my head. "No. I don't think it's necessary."

"Then your husband's body will be taken down to the morgue. After you contact a funeral home to make final arrangements, they will claim his body."

"Does that mean I have to find a funeral home myself? You guys don't do that?" I'd never handled anything like this before and didn't have the slightest idea how to proceed. Was I just supposed to call some random funeral home from the yellow pages, or did the hospital provide me with a list of places?

"No, we don't do that."

"Um, okay. I guess I'll figure it out."

"Perhaps the best thing would be to ask family or friends or maybe even your local church."

"That sounds like a good idea," I said, even though I knew I wouldn't be doing any of those things.

"Do you want me to get someone from social services to talk to you?" he asked.

I shook my head and wiped away a stray tear with the back of my hand. "No, I'll be fine."

Dr. Mallet walked away after that. It took a few minutes, but somehow I managed to collect my thoughts. There was a lot to do, and sitting around in an emergency room wasn't going to help get those things done. I had a funeral to plan. And a job. And kids that needed to be picked up from school in a few hours. I could sort through my feelings later when they were in bed for the night and the house was quiet. I stood up and headed back outside.

The first thing I did when I got home was call my supervisor, Diane. I worked as a human resources representative. Ninety-five percent of my job I was able to do from home. Only occasionally did I have to go into the office for meetings. But even though I didn't have an office I needed to show up to at a certain time, I still had emails and calls that needed answering. Which meant I had to speak to my supervisor and let her know what was going on.

"Oh my God," Diane said after I told her about Ryan. It felt so strange to say to someone that he'd died. "I'm so sorry. How are you holding up?"

I'd never been on the receiving end of condolences and wasn't really sure how to reply. "As well as can be expected."

"What happened?"

People were bound to ask me why my husband, at the age of thirty-five, was dead. I needed to get used to telling the story. So even though I didn't feel like talking about it, I explained that

Ryan had fallen asleep at the wheel on his way home from work.

"That's terrible. If there's anything I can do—"

"It's okay. I'll be fine. It's just that I'll probably fall behind on some of my tasks."

"Vanessa, that's the last thing you need to worry about right now. Take some time off, as much as you need."

"I'd rather not," I said. "Work is a good distraction." And provided a paycheck, which at that moment, I realized I'd need now more than ever with Ryan gone. A wave of panic ran through me. How was I supposed to take care of two kids and pay a mortgage on my income alone?

"Well, okay. If that's what you want. But if you change your mind, just shoot me an email."

"Thanks, Diane," I said.

I hung up the phone and sat down at my desk. Then I opened the web browser and typed "funeral homes Sacramento" in the search bar. A long list of options popped up. I clicked on the link at the top of the page. All of a sudden, I felt overwhelmed. There were too many choices, and I had no idea which was the right one. In the ten years we'd been married, Ryan and I had never talked about final arrangements. I didn't know if he wanted to be buried in a fancy satin-lined casket or if he preferred to be cremated. Would I have to plan a funeral service? Neither of us were churchgoers, so I had no idea how to get something like that arranged.

I turned away from the computer. I couldn't handle making a decision that big right then. Maybe someone in Ryan's family would know what to do. Not that there were many people to ask. Ryan's mother had passed away from breast cancer when he was a teenager. The only members of his family I'd ever met were his father and younger brother. Since he didn't get along with either of them, we didn't exactly keep in touch. I'd only met them a handful of times. Ryan used to call them freeloaders and complained that they only called when they needed something from him.

I sighed. That left the final-arrangements decision up to me. But not yet. I couldn't move forward with funeral plans until after I talked to the kids. Jacob was only nine, and Lydia only six. They were still so young. I was afraid of what losing their father would do to them. It was all I could think about, so before I did anything, I needed to let them know their daddy wasn't coming home anymore.

3

After picking Jacob and Lydia up from school, I listened to the two of them prattle on about their day. Just like I always did. In every way this day felt like any other. Except it wasn't. It struck me how innocent my children were. How completely oblivious they were to the shocking news I was about to unload on them. I wanted to put off telling them. Forever. But of course, that wasn't an option. So instead, I asked them to take a seat at the table as soon as we got home.

"We're skipping soccer practice today," I said.

"What? Why?" Jacob asked, sounding unhappy about it even though he usually grumbled about going.

"Because Mommy has something important that she needs to talk to you two about," I began, grasping their little hands in mine in an effort to comfort them and myself at the same time.

Jacob and Lydia looked up at me, their eyes full of curiosity. "What is it, Mommy?" Jacob asked, concern in his voice. He was such a sweet, sympathetic little boy.

I took a deep breath. "Your daddy got into an accident on his way home from work this morning."

"So that's why he wasn't home when we left for school?" Jacob asked.

"What kind of accident?" Lydia asked, her childlike voice as innocent sounding as she truly was.

"A car accident."

Jacob cocked his head to the side. "Is he okay?"

I shook my head and bit my lower lip, trying to keep myself from crying. I needed to be strong. "Your father was hurt very badly. He didn't make it."

Why couldn't I bring myself to just say the word dead? They were children. "He didn't make it" wasn't an expression kids typically understood. Or maybe it was. I had no way of actually knowing. This was all so new to me. I didn't know the right way to break the news to my children that their father was dead. Was there even a right way?

Lydia scrunched up her face. Her long hair was a mess like it always was after a day at school. She looked a lot like me, deep-brown hair, hazel eyes. Her brother, on the other hand, was a dirty blonde with brown eyes like his father's. "Make it where?"

"She means Daddy's dead," Jacob said to her before turning his head back toward me. "Right, Mom?"

That was my Jakey. He was a smart kid and proud of it too. Not that there was anything wrong with that.

"Wait, Daddy's dead?" Lydia asked, sounding more puzzled than anything.

I nodded. My throat had tightened to the point that I couldn't bring myself to reply with words.

"Are you sure?" Jacob asked.

I nodded again.

Jacob and Lydia glanced at each other. Almost in unison they began to cry. I pulled them both into my arms and let them sob into my shoulders. My heart bled for them. They were my everything. My whole world. Ever since Jacob had taken his first breath and let out his first cry, I'd fallen madly in love with him. Three years later, when his sister was born, it had been the same with her. Never in my wildest dreams had I imagined I could love anyone as much as I'd loved Ryan, but as soon as my children were born, everything changed. I didn't think a love as deep and profound as the love I had for my children even existed. I wanted to protect them from being hurt, and it killed me that I'd failed.

"So we'll never see him again?" Jacob managed to ask, his little voice cracking as he got the words out.

"I'm sorry, honey. But no." I squeezed him a little tighter. "He's with the angels now." I had no idea why I even said that. We weren't a religious family, but I hoped they'd find some comfort in those words.

"I'm scared, Mommy," Lydia said. "What if something happens to you too?"

"Oh, honey." I wiped her tears away with my fingertips. "Nothing will happen to me. I promise. I know how much you and your brother need me, and I won't ever leave you."

"You don't know that for sure," Jacob said, accusingly.

"Yes, I do," I replied, even though, of course, he was right. I couldn't really guarantee anything, but I'd do whatever was in my power to be there for them. "You have to trust me. Everything will be all right. I swear."

Jacob wiped his tear-soaked face with the back of his hand. "Is it okay if I go to my room?" He was nine and slowly starting to assert his independence. I hadn't expected it to happen so early, but I tried my best to give him the breathing room he wanted. Still, it worried me that he wanted to be on his own at a time like this.

"If you're sure that's what you want to do."

"I'm sure." He stood and headed down the hall toward his bedroom. I was tempted to follow him and make him talk, but when Jacob shut down, he didn't open back up until he was good and ready.

I carried Lydia in my arms over to the couch. At six, she was still small enough that I did that from time to time. Soon, she'd be too big. She lay her little head in my lap and started to cry again. I stroked her hair and whispered to her, "Everything will be all right."

After a while, she closed her eyes. All that crying had tired her out.

LATER THAT EVENING, while the kids were washing up right before bed, I managed to sneak in a call to my best friend, Marla. She was the one person I confided in about damn near everything because talking to her almost always made me feel better. I didn't want Jacob or Lydia to hear me discussing what happened to their dad on the phone, but I needed someone to talk to and figured the running water from the sink while the kids brushed their teeth would drown out the sound of my voice.

"Hey, girl," Marla said.

I took a deep breath. "Something terrible happened today."

"What?" Her tone had gone from casual to serious.

"Ryan died." It felt so strange to say those words. I choked back the lump in my throat. "He got into a car accident on his way home from work this morning."

"Holy crap, Vanessa," Marla said. "I don't even know what to say. I'm so sorry. What can I do?"

"There's nothing you can do," I said. "I just needed to tell someone."

"Do you want me to stop by?"

"No. You don't need to do that. I'll be fine."

She had her kids with her. Marla was a single mom, like I

now was, with two sons and a daughter of her own. She shared custody with her monster of an ex-husband, Steve, and Wednesdays were one of her days. Which meant she had three kids to help with homework, cook dinner for, and clean up after. Then she'd need to help them get ready for school the next day. I didn't want to add to her long list of things to do by having her drag her kids all the way over to my house. She didn't live that far away, but it was late, almost bedtime I realized as I glanced at the clock that hung on the wall in my kitchen. All things considered, I was doing better than I'd thought I would. After picking the kids up from school, I'd gone into Mommy mode, sorting out what I needed to do to help Jacob and Lydia get through losing their father. Everything else, my feelings about Ryan and being a widow, worrying about money, planning a funeral, was secondary. I was all they had now.

"Well, I'm coming over Friday with dinner. It's Steve's weekend with the kids," she said, "Don't even bother telling me no."

"Okay. I won't, then. Good night, Marla."

"You know I love you, right?"

"Yes." I smiled after hanging up, thankful that I had such a good friend, since when it came to family, I had very little to speak of. Strangely, that was one of the things Ryan and I had in common and something we'd bonded over when we'd first gotten together. We both knew how it felt to come from dysfunctional families. But after we fell in love, it didn't seem to matter. We'd said we'd be each other's family. If only it had actually worked out that way.

My parents split up when I was around Lydia's age. It happened not long after we'd moved from Los Angeles to Sacramento. My father hated it here. Sacramento was too small for him. He craved the big-city life he'd had back in Los Angeles. So one day he took off without a word. The next time my mother heard from him was a few months later, after he'd filed for a divorce. Like most people, a lot of my childhood memories had faded over the years, but not the one of my mother sobbing at the sight of those papers my father's lawyer had sent her.

I didn't even know where he was anymore. Maybe he was still in LA. For all I knew, he was long dead. My father's departure had left my mother so depressed that she couldn't function without the aid of some sort of prescription sedative or narcotic. Me and my brother, Brandon, had to learn how to take care of ourselves. As soon as he graduated from high school, he got the hell out of California. He finished his degree at some college in Illinois and never set foot in Sacramento again. Not even for my wedding. We talked on our birthdays and Christmas, which was about as often as I spoke to my mother, even though she only lived a half hour away in Citrus Heights.

That night, the kids slept in my bed, their bodies wrapped around me for comfort. I watched them while they slept, and for a few beautiful minutes, it felt like everything was going to be all right. I had them, and they had me, and I was good enough at the whole mom thing that I'd more than make up for the fact that their dad was gone. But then the doubts crept in. Just because Ryan and I had fallen apart didn't mean the kids felt the same way about their father as I did. He was Dad to them. And no matter how angry he sometimes made me, I wanted them to love him because I knew how much it hurt to not have a father in your life. That wasn't how Ryan saw things, though. Whenever the kids did anything to show they preferred me over him, Ryan insisted that I'd poisoned their minds against him, but he was wrong. I endlessly defended him, not for his sake, but for the children's.

"Kids are just naturally closer to their mother," I used to tell him every time he got upset when the kids fought over who got to sit next to me when we went out to eat.

"That's not true," he'd insist. "You just talk shit about me to them behind my back."

"Do you really have to start a fight with me right now? Can't we just enjoy lunch for once without you criticizing me?"

"You're the one who's criticizing me."

Back and forth it would go until I realized what we were doing. Ryan was either exceptionally good at baiting me, or I was exceptionally bad at not letting him get to me. When Jacob was first born, I'd sworn Ryan and I would never argue in front of our kids. Of course, back then things between us hadn't been as strained. I was still in love, happily bouncing away on my own personal cloud nine. At least most of the time.

I closed my eyes and pushed those memories out of my head. But that only made room for other thoughts. Like the argument Ryan and I had gotten into the afternoon before he'd died. He was so angry with me that he'd stormed out of the house, slamming the door behind himself as he left for work. I shook my head, not wanting to think about the words he'd used and the tone of voice he'd used them in.

As soon as I managed to stop thinking about that ugly blowup, my head filled with worries. How would we get by without Ryan's salary? He made more than I did. Way more. I knew he had life insurance and a retirement plan through work, but I doubted either of them would pay enough to make up for the loss of his income. Soon, hospital bills would start coming in. Ryan was a spender and had credit card debt that would need to be paid off. What would be left over after?

Suddenly ashamed of myself, I tried once more to steer my thoughts elsewhere. My husband had just died, and here I was, worrying about money instead of grieving over him. What kind of wife did that?

In the morning, I decided to keep the kids out of school. I called the school office and told the secretary that Jacob and

Lydia Collins would be absent for the rest of the week because their father had just passed away.

"Goodness gracious," she said. "How terrible. I'm so sorry for your loss."

"Thank you."

"Please let me know if there is anything we can do to help."

"We'll be fine," I said, trying to sound gracious while, at the same time, figuring out a way to get off the phone before she could ask any more questions. "I'm sorry but I ... I've gotta run."

I pressed the Hang Up button on my phone and sat down in front of the computer to email the kids' teachers.

By then, the kids were out of bed and had made their way into the kitchen.

"Won't we be late for school?" Lydia asked.

"You're not going today. Or tomorrow. I think you two need a little break and some Mommy time."

"But I have a math test on Friday," Jacob said.

"I just emailed your teacher. I'm sure they can reschedule it given—"

"That Daddy just died," Jacob said, finishing my sentence for me. He sounded so sad that my heart broke for him.

"Yes."

I waited for either of them to say something else about their father or ask me questions. I knew they had to have some, but instead Jacob poured bowls of cereal for himself and Lydia. That was new. Normally, he had to be asked to help his sister, and even then, he did it grudgingly. I wondered how long this would last.

FOR THE NEXT FEW DAYS, I did my best to distract the kids from the pain they had to be feeling by taking them for pizza and ice cream and to the movies. Not that it did much good. There were a lot of tears—mostly from Lydia because Jacob was trying his best to be tough—and neither of them felt like eating much. I knew their behavior was normal, but everything in me wanted to make things right for them with a snap of my fingers. If only life really worked that way.

On Friday evening, Marla came over. Jacob and Lydia's faces brightened as she stepped into the family room. I made popcorn, and we watched a movie. Halfway through it Jacob looked up at Marla, his expression shy and slightly pained. "Do you know what happened to my dad?" he practically whispered.

"I do, honey. And I'm so sorry." She hugged both of the kids. "You guys know if you ever need to talk to anyone, Auntie Marla is only a few doors away, right?"

Though she wasn't technically their aunt, sometimes it kind of felt like she was.

"We know," Jacob replied.

That night, after the kids went to bed, I worked myself up to calling my mother and brother. They did their best to sympathize, but my brother had never met Ryan, and my mother was too self-absorbed to truly care that her daughter was now a widow.

"Well, I managed to survive losing your father," she said.

I didn't bother to point out that our situations weren't really the same. True, she'd survived, but I prayed that I'd do a lot better of a job surviving than she had.

A WEEK LATER, when the kids were back in school, I'd finally made up my mind about Ryan's final arrangements. I hadn't succeeded in contacting either his father or brother. I'd looked through the contact list on Ryan's cell phone, but both his father's and brother's numbers were disconnected. I sent them emails, but neither replied. Facebook was another dead end.

Apparently, they weren't social-media users. With my lack of success in tracking down his family, I didn't see the point in a funeral. It wasn't like Ryan had an army of friends who wanted to pay their respects either. Cremation seemed like the best option.

I met with a funeral-home director who I'd talked to on the phone a few days earlier. She explained that I'd be given Ryan's ashes and showed me a catalog of urns they sold to keep them in, but I couldn't see myself placing Ryan's ashes in an urn on my fireplace mantel.

"You can always scatter the ashes if that's something you're more comfortable with."

I thought about it for a moment. "That sounds like a good idea, actually."

"You can't just scatter them anywhere, though. I'll give you a list of places to call to get more information on that."

Almost as soon as I finished signing the papers at the crematorium, I was hit with a wave of guilt. Did I choose cremation because it was the easiest and cheapest thing to do? Did I really think Ryan would be okay with it? He'd never told me he wanted a funeral and a burial, but what if he had and somehow expected that I'd just know that? He wasn't around to answer any of those questions, though, which left it up to me to decide.

At night, I tossed and turned in bed, thoughts of Ryan haunting me. He was gone, I told myself. He wouldn't know or care about what I decided to do ever again, so why did I feel so guilty about my choice to cremate his body? It was too late to change my mind. The papers had been signed and the fee paid out of the measly savings Ryan and I had accumulated. I just prayed I could live with the guilt.

4

A few days later, someone from the funeral home called to tell me Ryan's ashes were ready. I couldn't believe how fast things were moving. A part of me still couldn't truly accept that Ryan was gone. Less than two weeks ago, I'd been a wife. Now I was a widow and a single mother of two. It didn't seem impossible.

I texted Marla. She was only working a half day and made me promise to wait for her so I wouldn't have to be alone when I went to pick up Ryan's ashes.

At just after one, she rang the doorbell, and the two of us climbed into my car.

"How are you holding up?" she asked.

"Fine," I said. "I've been too busy to really have time to stop and think. You can't even begin to imagine all the paperwork involved after someone dies."

Over the past few days, I'd spent hours on the phone settling Ryan's credit card accounts. Every one of them needed a copy of his death certificate. Thank goodness I had a home office with a fax machine. Ryan's credit card accounts were only the tip of the iceberg, though. There was the hospital billing department and the ambulance service who'd brought him to the ER after his accident. The stack of bills I needed to pay seemed to grow by the day, but I couldn't take care of all those outstanding bills until I collected Ryan's life-insurance money, and that wasn't going to happen until I finished filling out the paperwork they sent me.

"What about Jake and Lydia? How are they doing?"

I shrugged. "It's hard to say. Lately, neither of them seems to want to talk about their dad." I glanced at her. "Do you think that's normal?"

"I don't know. Your kids are a million times closer to you than they ever were to Ryan."

"He's still their dad, though. They have to be feeling something. I just wish they'd tell me what."

"Have you asked them?"

I shook my head. "Not directly."

"Maybe you should."

Marla was right. The problem was that over the past few years, I'd gotten good at avoiding conflict, at not talking about feelings and instead burying my head in the sand. It was the only way to survive the kind of marriage I had. What good was talking about your feelings when nothing ever changed?

"I was planning on having a small funeral service outside in our backyard before scattering Ryan's ashes. I figured it would give the kids a chance to talk about their feelings."

"That sounds like a great idea."

I glanced at Marla out of the corner of my eye. Her long honey-blond hair was pulled back into a neat ponytail. "Do you think you could come?"

"If you need me to be there, then I will be." She leaned back in her seat.

A few minutes later, as I pulled into the funeral home parking lot, I noticed a weird grin on her face.

"What are you smiling about?" I asked.

She shook her head. "It's so wrong of me to say this, but I was just thinking that it's a good thing Ryan is already dead, because he would just die if he knew I was coming to his funeral."

Marla was right about that. It would be an understatement to say she and Ryan had never got along. They both absolutely loathed each other. "Well, it's not really a funeral."

"Oh, you know what I mean."

Before I could stop myself, I laughed. And then I laughed some more. Marla joined in, which just made me laugh even harder. She was right. Ryan would hate that she was coming to his memorial service. He despised Marla because he hated anything or anyone that took attention or time from him. Marla loathed him right back, mostly because she was my best friend and she thought I deserved better than him. Perhaps I did, but when you have children with someone, your lives become irrevocably intertwined. I couldn't just walk away, no matter how many times I felt like I really wanted to.

I pulled myself together. It would not be good to walk into a funeral home laughing. Truthfully, there was nothing funny about this situation, but sometimes, when things got too overwhelming, that's what I did. I laughed at the absurdity of life and the way it never failed to throw a curve ball when I least expected one.

After signing a few more papers, I was handed Ryan's ashes, which had been placed in a sturdy cardboard box. As I stared down at it, I did my best to push away the wave of guilty thoughts that plowed toward me. There was nothing funny about Ryan being dead. I felt terrible about laughing at what Marla had said earlier in the car. It was wrong for me to feel anything but sad at a time like this.

People told me all the time that I thought too much. They

were right, but I couldn't help it. Maybe it was because I hadn't had the easiest of lives. All that was supposed to change when Ryan and I fell in love. He was handsome and sweet, or at least he had been in the beginning. We bonded over the many things we had in common like the fact that we were both finishing up our college degrees even though we were in our mid-twenties. Or that we both came from broken families. I'd convinced myself that we were destined to be together. What an idiot I'd been back then.

As I pulled into Marla's driveway, she put her hand on my shoulder. "You do know that it's still okay to laugh every now and then, right?"

I smiled at her. "Thanks, Marla."

One of the reasons I loved her so much was because she got me, even though, in many ways, she was my complete opposite. Her house was total chaos, and she seemed to revel in that. I was sort of a neat freak who'd sweep and mop my floors until not a speck of dirt was left behind. Of the two of us, I was the serious one, while Marla was the ball of energy.

She gave me a hug before hopping out of the car. I drove off and headed to the kids' school to pick them up. I didn't say anything to them about their dad's ashes being in the trunk. The idea of it sort of freaked me out, and I was an adult. I could only imagine what two kids would think about sharing a car ride with their dead father's ashes.

Over dinner, I told them about my plan to have a memorial service for their dad on Saturday and, after, take Ryan's ashes and scatter them in one of the parks near our home.

"Will it just be the three of us?" Jacob asked.

"Marla's coming over too," I said. I'd contemplated asking my mom to come, but the kids weren't really comfortable around her.

"Will we have to touch the ashes?" Lydia asked.

"Of course not. In fact, if you prefer not to come along for that part, you can always stay back at the house with Marla."

"No, we want to go with you," Jacob said.

"Yeah," Lydia chimed in.

That night, while I lay in bed, I couldn't help but wonder, yet again, if I'd made a mistake. Maybe having Ryan buried in a local cemetery would have been better. But it was too late for that. Still, I couldn't stop picturing the frightened look on Lydia's face when I'd talked about scattering Ryan's ashes. Lots of people did it, but lots of people also kept ashes in beautiful urns on their mantel pieces. Should I have just chosen that option? For some reason the idea of keeping cremated remains in my house made me feel ill. And leaving them in the garage just seemed wrong.

In the end, I decided it was better to move forward with my plan. Changing it would just confuse the kids. And that was the last thing I wanted to do.

5

On a cold late-January Saturday afternoon, Marla came over with a lasagna and a pie. It was her ex-husband's weekend with their kids, so she'd spent the morning cooking a meal for us. I hugged her, touched by her thoughtfulness. Having almost no family to speak of made it easy to appreciate my friends that much more.

I put the lasagna in the fridge. "Am I crazy for doing this?" I asked Marla.

She shook her head. "I don't think so."

We joined Jacob and Lydia in the family room. "Are you guys ready?"

"Ready for what?" Lydia asked, staring at the TV instead of me.

"We're going to say goodbye to Daddy," I reminded her. It was the best way I knew how to explain what was going on to my six-year-old.

Jacob turned the TV off. "C'mon," he said to his sister.

With the box that held Ryan's ashes in my hands, I headed to the backyard. Marla and the kids trailed behind me. Earlier I'd set a giant beach blanket down on the grass. The four of us took a seat on it.

"The reason I wanted to have this gathering was to give you both a chance to talk about your dad. Maybe there's things you want to get off your chest, or some words you might want to say in his honor."

Marla put her arm over Jakey's shoulder, then she reached for Lydia's hand. "Sometimes it's good to talk about your feelings."

Jacob shrugged his shoulders. "I can't really think of anything to say." He wasn't much for words, but it troubled me that he didn't want to say anything. He had to be feeling *something* about losing his father. Why was it so hard for him to put his thoughts into words?

"I'm sorry you're gone, Daddy," Lydia said, her voice soft. "I really miss you."

I struggled to come up with a few words of my own. I tried reaching into my mind for happier memories of Ryan. Like the day he finally got me that engagement ring he'd promised. It was gorgeous, and he was so proud to give it to me. A month later we exchanged vows in front of a small group of friends. The only family either of us had in attendance was my mother, who'd shown up stoned from her anxiety pills.

I remembered waking up on the morning of our wedding, petrified that I was making a huge mistake, but I refused to listen to that voice. I'd lost count of how many times I looked back on that day, full of regret.

I sighed. It was hard to find a happy memory of Ryan because every single one I had was overshadowed by remorse and anger with myself for not listening to my gut all those years ago. The only thing that made up for the nightmare our marriage turned out to be was the kids Ryan and I had had together. They were the only good thing that had come out of our cursed union.

"Your daddy loved the two of you so much," I said. "He might not have always been good at showing it, but he really did. I know that you're both sad he's gone, so if you ever want to talk to me and tell me how you're feeling, I want you to know that I'll listen."

"And I will too," Marla added.

"I just hope that wherever Daddy is right now, that at least he's happy," Jacob said, his voice barely above a whisper.

Apparently, even my nine-year-old had come to realize how deeply unsatisfied with life Ryan was. Was he blaming himself, as I often did, for Ryan's unhappiness? I would have to ask him about that later. Maybe he'd feel more comfortable talking about his feelings if it was just the two of us.

"I think he is," I said. "I know he misses you guys, but he's looking down on the two of you, and he's proud that you're being so brave."

For a moment it looked like Jacob was going to say something else, but he must've changed his mind because, instead, he lowered his head and stared at his hands, which were folded in his lap. Lydia also sat quietly. This "service" was supposed to be their opportunity to talk about their feelings, yet both my children were alarmingly silent. I looked at Marla who just gave me a shrug.

After another few minutes of trying to get my kids to open up, I finally decided it was time to head back inside. Jacob and Lydia happily agreed.

"Are you two still sure you want to come with me? You can stay here with Marla if you prefer."

"We want to go with you," Lydia insisted.

"Can Marla come too?" Jacob asked.

I glanced at Marla who nodded. A few minutes later, we

piled into the car. I looked at my kids' faces through my rearview mirror. Jacob had a blank look on his face, and tears streamed down Lydia's. A hopeless feeling settled over me. Seeing their sad faces was like a knife to my heart.

The kids remained quiet as I discreetly scattered their father's ashes in a park just a few miles from our house. I wasn't even sure that what I was doing was entirely legal since California had so many laws, but the deed was quickly done, and in less than an hour, we were back in the car. The kids' faces remained stony until we returned home. Once we did, they planted themselves in front of the TV while Marla helped me in the kitchen.

"Some kids aren't good at talking about their feelings," she said while I pulled plates from the cabinet to serve the lasagna on. "If you're worried, I can give you the name of the therapist I took my kids to after the divorce."

"Do you think therapy helped them?"

"It's hard to say. After Steve and I split up, my kids were like yours are now. Mostly quiet. I swore they were fine until their report cards came home. That's when I started taking them to counseling. But things might be different with Jakey and Lydia. It hasn't been that long since Ryan died. Maybe they're just not ready to open up yet."

LATER THAT EVENING, after Lydia fell asleep, I went into Jacob's bedroom. He was busy playing with his Legos and didn't even look up when I came in.

"Hey, honey, is it okay if we talk for a bit?"

"Sure."

I sat on his bed and patted the empty spot beside me. "Come sit."

He put down his Legos and joined me on his bed.

"Earlier, when you said you hoped Daddy was happy, what did you mean by that?"

Jacob shrugged. "He was always so mad or sad all the time. I felt sorry for him."

I put my hand on Jacob's shoulder. "But you do know that wasn't your fault, right?"

For a moment he looked doubtful. "I guess," he finally said.

There were words at the tip of my tongue, but I didn't say them. I worried that they'd come out wrong, that it would sound like I was criticizing Ryan. The kids didn't need to hear that. They needed encouragement. I kissed the top of Jacob's head. "You know Mommy loves you, right?"

He looked up at me. "Yeah."

After I left Jacob's room, I thought about what Marla had said earlier. Maybe she was right. Maybe it was too soon for the kids to talk about their feelings. Which meant there was nothing I could do but wait for them to come to me whenever they were ready.

6

For the first two weeks after Ryan died, it almost felt like he was just away, camping with friends or visiting family, which was weird, because he didn't actually do those types of things. Still, I half expected him to walk in the door and tell me how happy he was to finally be home.

Hours later, or days, if I was lucky, his mood would turn. He'd bark at me that he knew I wasn't happy he was home, that me and the kids never wanted him around anyway, so he might as well just turn right back around and leave again.

I'd sigh and plead with him to stay, and of course he would, since Ryan almost never actually made good on his threats. Still, the whole thing was just so tiring.

But as more weeks passed, it finally hit me that Ryan was really and truly gone. I went through his belongings, emptying out his half of the closet and dresser and filling boxes with clothes to take to Goodwill. I came across a stack of pictures from when the two of us had just started dating. We'd done so much together back then. Like spent weekends exploring the beach in Monterey or sledding in Tahoe. Ryan had piles of those pictures in one of his dresser drawers. In each one, I'd had a smile on my face. How had we gone from that to being so miserably unhappy with each other?

A part of me wanted to cry, to mourn my broken heart and crushed spirit, but I had no tears left. In my own way, I'd mourned Ryan years ago when I realized he'd never change. Every insult and accusation left my heart so wounded that I finally had no choice but to harden it, letting it freeze inside my chest to stop the pain. With a shake of my head, I brushed those thoughts away. I refused to let myself become consumed with anger and bitterness.

I looked through Ryan's letters and pictures one more time and came to the realization that they were of no use to me. I had no reason to hold on to them, so despite the echo of Ryan's voice in my head telling me what an awful person I was for doing it, I threw them in the trash.

Life as a single mother should've felt stranger, and harder, but Ryan hadn't been a particularly helpful husband. He barely washed dishes. Occasionally, he put clothes in the washing machine, but he never folded them or put them away. His income as an X-ray tech was his main contribution to the household. If he wasn't at work or sleeping, he was either in front of the TV, playing a game on his phone, or complaining to me about one thing or another. I knew so many women who grumbled that their husbands were never home, but for me, life was actually easier when Ryan wasn't around. That hadn't changed with his death. And I felt horrible for thinking that way.

Guilt gnawed at me all the time. I was supposed to miss my husband, not be relieved that he was gone. I couldn't help but wonder what the kids would think of me if they knew. They'd probably hate me, and how could I blame them? So I kept my thoughts to myself, bottling them up and tucking them away.

I went back to full-time work, fitting in a few hours of phone calls and catching up with emails while the kids were in school and then a few hours of paperwork after picking them up. I'd never really fallen in love with my job, but it was a good escape from the rollercoaster ride of emotions I cycled through on a daily basis.

Days turned into weeks then weeks into months. Somehow, two of them passed after Ryan's death. I struggled to cut back on expenses and even thought about putting our house on the market, but moving to a cheaper neighborhood meant the kids would have to change schools, and I didn't want them to have to go through that. Losing their father was a big enough life-changing event. Asking them to adjust to a new house and a new school so soon after was too much.

Ryan and I had talked about upgrading to a bigger house. At just over twelve hundred square feet, our extremely outdated three-bedroom, single-story ranch-style house had felt tiny when it had been the four of us. With Ryan gone, it didn't feel so small. Our house needed to be remodeled, but with only one income, my dreams of hardwood floors and granite countertops would have to wait.

One afternoon, just after I'd scarfed down a quick lunch, Marla texted me.

Want to go to the gym?

I hadn't been since Ryan died.

Can't. I've got too much to do. :(

I'm not taking no for an answer. Be ready in ten minutes.

I sighed. Though life had fallen back into somewhat of a routine, there was no denying that things had changed. Sorting through household finances ate up more time than I wanted it to. I avoided the mom crew at the kids' school and soccer practices because I'd grown tired of answering questions about Ryan. I never got out of the car anymore when I dropped the kids off at school or picked them up, choosing instead to wait in my car for them rather than deal with a bunch of nosy moms who normally wouldn't pay me an ounce of attention. And I found myself spending more time with the kids in an effort to make up for their dad being gone. It left very little me time. Marla worried that I wasn't taking care of myself, which was probably why she was trying to lure me to the gym.

Maybe a workout would do me some good, help me clear my head a bit. Exercise had been my stress reliever in the past. Before Ryan died, I went to the gym every morning right after dropping the kids off at school. Once I finished my workout, I felt energized and ready to tackle the pile of work waiting for me at home. Marla was right. Not taking care of myself wasn't going to solve my problems.

True to her word, Marla showed up ten minutes later. I'd just finished putting my socks on when the doorbell rang.

"Come in," I shouted from my bedroom.

"Good, you're dressed," she said as I walked into the family room moments later.

"We've got kids that need picking up in less than two hours," I said, looking at my phone to check the time, "so we better get going." I grabbed a bottle of water from the refrigerator and swung my gym bag over my shoulder.

The gym was only a five-minute drive from my house. When we got there, Marla and I deposited our belongings into a locker and headed toward the cardio room. On the way there, as I glanced down at my phone to search for my favorite music app, I heard someone call my name.

I lifted my head and found myself face-to-face with a man it took me a few moments to recognize. "Alex?" I asked, my eyes widening. "Alex Brooks?"

"You remember," he said.

"Of course I do." I was practically bubbling over with excitement, but I didn't want him to know that. "What are you doing here?"

I hadn't seen him since junior year of high school. He and his family had up and moved to Pollock Pines halfway through the year. I remembered how upset I'd been when he told me they were leaving. It wasn't even that far away, but in high school, an hour's drive seemed like an eternity. We'd kept in touch for a little while but eventually drifted apart. That was way before Facebook was a thing.

"I moved back down this way," he said.

I realized I was staring at him and quickly turned my head to look at Marla. "Marla, this is Alex. Alex, Marla." She gave him a quick handshake.

"Nice to meet you."

"We went to high school together," I explained.

"Cool," Marla said, glancing down at her watch.

I picked up on Marla's hint. Even though I wanted to stick around and talk to him some more, I couldn't really think of anything to say. "It was nice seeing you, Alex," I said. "But if Marla and I don't get started now, we'll be late picking our kids up from school."

"It was nice seeing you too." He leaned in for a hug, and I flashed back to another time, when the two of us had been close. I missed those days. My heart did a funny little thud in my chest. "Hopefully, I'll see you around," he said.

"He's cute," Marla said as I followed her over to the treadmills.

I looked them over tentatively. "You know what? It's been a while since I've ran. I think I'm going to start out on the elliptical instead."

I walked away and found an empty machine. Then I popped earbuds into my ears and started pumping away. A few minutes into my workout, I was so zoned out that I didn't notice Alex standing right next to me until he tapped my shoulder.

I pulled my earbuds out.

"Hey," he said. "I know you're in a rush, but I was sort of hoping we could exchange numbers. I'd really like to catch up with you. Maybe we could grab a cup of coffee sometime?"

I hadn't expected an invitation to hang out, so I just stared at him instead of replying.

He looked embarrassed. "Just as friends. I know you're married and all. I didn't mean to make it sound like I was asking you out."

I glanced down at my hand. It had never occurred to me to take off my wedding ring.

"Don't worry about it," I teased, reaching for my phone. "I honestly didn't think you were hitting on me."

His expression softened. I added his name to my contact list and handed him my phone so he could punch in his number.

"I'll text you so you can have my number," I said after he gave it back to me.

"Okay, well I guess I'll let you get back to it."

I looked over my shoulder as he walked away. It had been almost twenty years since I'd seen Alex Brooks. The crazy thing was, he looked just as good now as he had in high school. A few things had changed. His shoulders had broadened quite a bit—it was obvious he was a regular at the gym. And he had a few lines around his periwinkle-blue eyes. In every other way, he looked the same. He still had thick dark-brown hair that showed no sign of thinning or graying, but it was his smile that I remembered the most. It hadn't changed a bit. It lit up his face and made his eyes sparkle. Half the girls in high school had a huge crush on him, including me. I'd never told him, though. I liked having him as a friend and didn't want to screw that up by telling him how I felt.

As I pedaled away, I couldn't help but wonder what his story was. Was he married? I hadn't bothered to look at his hand for a ring. Did he have kids?

Twenty minutes later, I finished with the elliptical and hopped onto a stationary bike. Marla walked over and took the empty machine beside me.

"So what did he want?" she asked, her brows raised.

"Just to see if I wanted to catch up sometime."

She grinned. "You want to know what I think?"

"Sure."

"I say go for it. He's *really* handsome."

I frowned. "He wasn't asking me out on date." Even if he had been, I would've definitely said no. I had no room in my life for a relationship. High school was a long time ago. I might have had a crush on him back in those days, but a lot had changed since then.

"What's his story anyway?"

"We were friends in high school, but then he moved, and we lost touch. I haven't seen him in years." I paused to think about what a strange coincidence it was. "It's so weird that I ran into him here of all places."

We pedaled for a few more minutes without talking. Marla slowed her pace and glanced at me. "So how are you holding up?"

"Me? I'm fine."

She asked me that same question at least a few times a week, and every time I gave her the same answer.

"You don't seem fine," she replied.

I furrowed my brows. "What do you mean by that?"

She shrugged. "I don't know. It's just that you seem kind of ... lost."

"Lost?" At first the description seemed strange, but the more I thought about it, the more I realized that the word fit. It was how Lydia and Jacob seemed half the time. I'd been asking them almost on a daily basis how they were, and their answers were always the same. They were fine.

I didn't believe them any more than Marla believed me.

"You know me," she said. "I'm not one to sugarcoat things."

I sighed. "Sometimes I wonder if it would've been easier to go through all this if Ryan and I had a better relationship."

"What do you mean by that?"

"I'm supposed to be missing my dead husband, but the truth is, mostly I don't. Sometimes I'm even kind of glad he's gone. And I feel like a terrible person for thinking that way." There I'd said it. Getting the words out felt like cutting out the rotten flesh of an infected appendage. Those thoughts had been eating at me for the past two months. Along with what Ryan had said to me the day before he died. But that was a conversation I couldn't bring myself to share with anyone. Some days I could barely look at myself in the mirror. But despite the guilt that gnawed at me almost constantly, I had no choice but to keep myself together for the kids. It was a delicate balancing act.

"I was so waiting for you to finally say that." Marla put her hand on my arm. "You need to stop feeling terrible for being human. Let's just face it. Ryan was kind of an asshole. No one would blame you for feeling the way you do."

A part of me knew she was right, but I couldn't shake the voice in my head that kept whispering that I was a toxic person and that everything that had gone wrong between Ryan and me was actually my fault. On some level, I knew it wasn't, but it was hard to get the things Ryan had said to me over the past few years out of my head. "Asshole or not, he's my children's father. I can tell they miss him. And if they knew what I was thinking, they'd probably hate me for it."

"There's no reason for them to know how you felt about their dad. I *hate* Steve, but I'd never tell my kids that."

"That's different. Steve isn't dead."

"It's not your fault that Ryan got into a car accident."

"But what if it is? What if he was so upset over our last argument that he was too distracted to drive safely?"

Ironically, it was Marla we'd been fighting over.

"You spend too much time with her," he'd said to me only hours before he'd left for work.

"She's my friend, and her kids are friends with ours. There's nothing wrong with that."

"You're trying to cut me out of your life."

"No, I'm not," I insisted.

"If you don't want me around, I'll just leave. You'd like that, wouldn't you?" He was shouting so loudly I was worried the kids would overhear. They hated when the two of us argued.

I stared into Ryan's angry eyes, trying to keep my temper in check. "I'm not going to argue with you." I walked away, angry and annoyed because this wasn't the first time Ryan complained about me spending time with my friends instead of him. I didn't have the nerve to tell him that I'd rather spend time with just about anyone else but him. He wouldn't take that well.

Instead of backing off, Ryan had followed me. He wasn't ready to stop yelling. Now, I sighed, trying to push his words and my reply to them out of my head.

Marla gave me a stern look. "Don't do that to yourself. That accident was *not* your fault."

"I should have insisted he switch to the day shift," I said, even though I doubted that would've made a difference.

"Didn't you tell me he liked working nights?"

"He didn't like working at all. If he had his way, we'd be on vacation every day."

"With what money?"

I shrugged. "I don't know. I said that to him at least a hundred times." Not that it had done much good. Ryan lived in a fantasy world where people took expensive vacations whenever they wanted, husbands and wives had sex every day, children always obeyed their parents, and people got to buy every damn thing they wanted. Reality left him bitter and angry and caused more arguments between us than I cared to remember.

More than once I'd asked Ryan to stop working nights. The lack of sleep made his anger worse and him impossible to be around, but he refused. He kept saying that he made more money working nights and there were less people to deal with overnight than during the day. But my attempts to get him to switch to day shift were half-hearted at best. A part of me liked that he worked night shifts because it meant I got the bed to myself for a few days every week. I loved not having to wake up to him pressing his morning boner into me, hopeful that somehow it was enough to get me so turned on that I'd rip my clothes off and make crazy passionate love to him. It didn't matter to him if the kids were awake or even knocking on the door. "They can wait," he'd whisper in my ear. Ugh.

"That's exactly what I'm talking about. Ryan didn't always make the best decisions. That's on him, not you."

I gave Marla a weak smile. She was trying to help, but she could only do so much. I didn't want to be drowning in guilt and shame, but not wanting something didn't keep it from happening.

Fifteen minutes later, we finished up on the stationary bikes. We headed to the weight room to work on our arms for a bit before getting our things from the locker room.

On our way back to Marla's car, she said, "I was thinking of asking Lynette over on Friday. It's my weekend with the kids, so I thought we could do another one of our girls'-slash-game nights at my house. What do you think?"

I hadn't seen Lynette in a long time. She'd sent flowers after Ryan died, and we'd texted a few times. She was as good a friend as Marla, only I didn't see her as often because she lived farther away and worked long hours. Game night with Marla's and

Lynette's kids would be fun for Jacob and Lydia, and if there was one thing they were sorely lacking, it was having fun.

"I think it's a great idea. It feels like forever since we've gotten together."

"Awesome. I'll text you the details after I talk to Lynette."

"That sounds great," I said, managing a smile. For weeks my life had been consumed with funeral planning, settling Ryan's affairs, my job, and being a mother. It had literally been months since the kids and I had done something fun together with friends. It felt nice to have something to look forward to.

7

S ince I still lived in the same city I'd gone to high school in, I sometimes ran into old acquaintances. We'd make small talk, exchange numbers, and promise to keep in touch, but it never actually happened. The most I'd get was a friend request on Facebook, so I hadn't actually expected to hear from Alex. When he texted me the next day, it took me by surprise.

After a bit of back and forth, Alex and I settled on a time and place to meet. All that day, my heart fluttered in my chest in a funny way. I tried ignoring it. When that didn't work, I chalked it up to anxiety, which plagued me from time to time. It could not be Alex that had me feeling that way. For one thing, I hadn't seen him in forever. And for all I knew, he was nothing like the Alex I'd known in high school all those years ago. Even if he wasn't married, which I highly doubted since a guy like him was bound to have been scooped up by some gorgeous, supermodel-looking woman, I'd only been a widow for two months. There was no way I could even think about dating so soon after Ryan's death.

I thought back to the times Ryan had asked me if I planned

to move on with someone else after he died. I never quite understood the purpose of such a question, but I played along anyway.
When we first got together, I thought his jealous streak was kind
of cute—it meant he truly loved me—but over the years I'd
grown to hate it. After ten years and two kids together, he was
almost as insecure as he had been in the beginning of our relationship. I used to insist that if he died, I'd be lost without him,
that I'd be too heartbroken to move on with anyone else, but
he'd just tell me I was lying. Ryan was so self-absorbed that he
never stopped to think about how hurtful that was, to be called a
liar by the person I loved, but that was his way. *Everything* was
about him and his feelings. After a while, I started tuning him
out, refusing to let him bait me. But he hated being ignored.
He'd push and push until he got some kind of reaction out
of me.

I sighed, trying to shake those memories out of my head.
Instead, I thought about Jacob and Lydia and the way they'd
smiled the day before, when I'd told them about game night at
Marla's. I'd missed seeing them smile. The thought pinched
my heart.

FRIDAY NIGHT COULD NOT COME FAST ENOUGH. When it finally
rolled around, I ordered pizzas to bring to Marla's.

"Have you guys picked out which games you want to bring
with you?" I called out over my shoulder after paying the pizza
delivery guy.

Jacob bounded down the hallway with *Apples to Apples* in
his hands.

"You think we can watch this at Marla's?" Lydia handed me a
Backyardigans DVD.

"No one wants to watch that baby show," Jacob said.

"Hey," I said, irritated. "Don't talk to your sister like that."

Jacob scowled at me but didn't say another word. I walked a fine line with him and Lydia. If I didn't reprimand Jacob for being unkind, Lydia would get mad at me for not saying anything, but then Jacob would accuse me of favoring his sister because she was a girl and the youngest. This parenting thing was hard, and doing it alone was wearying. Not that it had been much different when Ryan was alive. Unlike most moms I knew, I didn't have girls' nights out without the kids or take vacations with my friends. The kids protested when I left them at home alone with their dad, and the truth was I liked being around them more than I liked taking time for myself. Soon enough, they'd be all grown up and out of the house. I wanted to enjoy the time I had with them before it was too late.

"We're supposed to be having fun tonight. That means no fighting, you two."

"We won't," Lydia chimed in innocently.

I gave them the mom stare, the look that told them I expected good behavior from them. Then, with pizza in hand, the three of us marched over to Marla's house. The entrance of her home opened up into a great room with a kitchen, dining table, and family room in one large area. Lynette and her daughter, Isabel, were already there. They both greeted me with hugs. Jacob and Lydia ran over to the couch to join the other kids who were in the middle of watching *Teen Titans*.

"Girl, it feels like it's been forever." Lynette got up from the dining table to give me a hug and cheek kiss.

It really had been. I hadn't seen her since before Ryan had died. Lynette was a doctor, so she worked *a lot*.

"I got some hard lemonade if you're interested," Marla called out from the kitchen area.

"Bring it on." I grabbed a slice of pizza while Marla fished out drinks from the refrigerator and placed them on the kitchen island.

"So how have you been?" Lynette asked.

"Hanging in there," I replied. "What about you?"

"I'm good. Been busy at work, but other than that, life's pretty much been the same."

"How's Bobby doing?" I rarely saw her husband. He wasn't much into socializing, but at least he didn't seem to mind that Lynette enjoyed it.

She shrugged. "He's good, I guess." Lynette and Bobby didn't have the best of marriages, and most of the time she preferred not talking about her husband at all. Sometimes it felt like more people I knew had bad marriages than good ones. Which was just one more reason I resolved to never ever return to the dating scene.

Teen Titans must've ended because, all of a sudden, the kids ran to the table and started grabbing slices of pizza.

Marla walked over to us with a big plate of brownies in her hands. "You guys can have *one* when you're done with pizza. Do you hear me? Just one."

"Just one?" her daughter, Abby, groaned.

"Is there an echo in here?" Marla asked, playfully looking around the room. Her gaze stopped at Abby. "I cut them really big. Trust me, one will be more than enough for you."

I smiled, realizing how much I missed these get-togethers of ours and how much I'd missed my friends' children. Over the years, we'd spent so much time around each other that they almost felt like family. And this time, my phone wouldn't be ringing every ten minutes with calls or texts asking me when I planned on coming back home. Ryan hated when I spent time with anyone but him. And since he disliked Marla so much, he never came along when I went to her house. Not having to answer to him felt like a weight off my shoulders.

After the kids finished eating, they went back to the family room to play. Marla looked across the table at Lynette. "So, did Vanessa tell you her big news?"

"What big news?" Lynette asked.

"Good question," I said. "I have no idea what Marla's talking about."

"Vanessa ran into some hottie she went to high school with at the gym the other day, and he asked her out."

I shook my head. "Whoa, wait just one minute. Yes, I ran into an old friend, but he did not ask me out. He thinks I'm married, and for all I know, he is too."

"Why does he think you're married?" Lynette asked, inquisitively.

I glanced down at my hand and started fiddling with my wedding band.

"You're still wearing it?" Lynette asked, her brows raised.

"I really hadn't thought about taking it off."

"I think you should," Marla said. "You're never going to meet a guy wearing that thing."

I narrowed my eyes at her. "Well, that's fine. Because I'm not interested in meeting guys."

"Maybe not right now, but someday you might be," Lynette said, pulling her sleek dark hair back into a ponytail.

I shook my head. "I can't even think about that right now. Which means that even if Alex is single, having coffee with him won't be a date. It'll just be two old friends catching up and talking about old times. That's all."

"If you say so." Marla took a swig from her bottle of hard lemonade.

I knew Marla well enough to know she was only kidding around about Alex. She got some strange thrill out of eliciting reactions from people, and despite her own failed marriage, she was an insatiable romantic.

"Mommy," Lydia called out. "Can you come play with us?"

The kids had *Apples to Apples* set up on the coffee table.

"Sure, I'd love to," I said, getting up from the table. Anything to get away from talking about why I was still wearing my wedding band and if I ever planned on dating again.

ALL THAT WEEKEND, I couldn't stop thinking about Alex and what we'd talk about when we met for coffee. He already knew I had kids since I'd mentioned them when I ran into him at the gym, but he'd probably ask how many. And he'd ask what my husband was like, which meant I'd have to tell him about Ryan's accident. Maybe Alex would also wonder why I was still wearing my wedding ring. Maybe a lot of people wondered that. I wasn't married anymore, it made no sense to keep wearing it.

I stared at my reflection in the mirror above my bedroom dresser and ran a hand through my hair. I was only thirty-five, and thanks to my obsessive use of sunscreen, a lot of people told me I looked younger. I was definitely not as beautiful as I had been in my twenties, but I still got my fair share of compliments. It didn't matter, though. I had no desire to date again. Maybe that's why I'd kept my wedding ring on. But with Ryan gone, it made no sense to keep wearing it.

I glanced down at my hand then slid my wedding band off my finger. As I did, a pang of guilt stabbed me in my gut. I held the ring in the palm of my hand. It was a simple platinum band. I'd stopped wearing my fancy engagement ring after giving birth because the stone seemed to catch on everything, and I worried about damaging the prongs. For a moment I contemplated switching the ring to my right hand, but in the end, I opened up my jewelry box and placed my wedding band beside my engagement ring.

The nauseous feeling in my stomach stayed with me the rest of the day. So did the anxiety that came along with it. For some reason, it suddenly hit me that I was really and truly alone in this world. My marriage to Ryan hadn't been great. At times it was even miserable, but he was still my husband. What would I do if I got sick? Who would take care of me and the kids? The thought filled me with panic. Ryan had a lot of flaws, but he wasn't all bad. A few years back, I'd had to have my appendix removed. I couldn't lift anything heavy for the first few days after my surgery, so he was the one who took care of the kids and helped me around the house while I recovered. If I needed help now, who would I ask?

Worrying wouldn't solve anything. But just like so many other nights, I couldn't turn my thoughts off and had to resort to taking something to help me sleep.

8

On Monday, right after dropping the kids at school, I drove to a coffee shop a few blocks from my house. Alex was already waiting for me and stood as soon as he saw me walk inside.

"Hey," he said, greeting me with a hug. Once more, my heart thumped in my chest.

"Hi," I said back.

"I've got to go to work later," he said, apparently noticing that I'd been taking in his appearance. He was dressed in worn jeans and a faded T-shirt but somehow managed to look more handsome than he had just a few days earlier.

"Oh yeah? Where do you work?"

"For the local electric company. I'm a lineman."

That explained his attire. And those strong shoulders, which I couldn't help but notice again.

"Should we get some coffee?" I asked. What a dumb question. Of course, we should get coffee. We were in a coffee shop after all.

"Yeah, of course."

We got in line, Alex in front of me. "What do you like to drink?"

"I'll get a small mocha."

When we got to the cashier, he ordered for us then turned his head to ask, "Nothing to eat?"

I shook my head. He paid for our drinks, then we sat back down, waiting for the barista to call out our names.

"So, how have you been?" Alex asked.

"Good," I said, feeling a sudden rush of nerves. All weekend, at least a dozen different questions I planned on asking Alex had run through my mind, but now, sitting across from him, I'd forgotten them all.

Alex leaned back in his chair. "How long has it been?"

"Almost twenty years," I replied, still not quite believing it had been that long. It hardly seemed possible.

"Yeah, I think eighteen to be exact." Alex shook his head. "And you look the same. Your hair's a bit shorter, but that's about it."

That was definitely not it. Thanks to two pregnancies and way too much stress eating, I was also at least thirty pounds heavier than I'd been in high school, but I wasn't about to point that out to him. "You do too."

The barista called Alex's name. When he returned with our coffees, he said, "Tell me what's been going on with you." He added sugar and half and half to his coffee. "How long have you been married? How many kids do you have?"

I braced myself for his reaction before beginning. "Well, technically I'm not married anymore." I knew this would come up. I just hadn't expected it to come up so soon.

"Oh?"

Maybe it was better to just get it out of the way. "Ryan, that was my husband's name, he passed away a little over two months ago."

Alex's mouth formed a perfect O. "What happened?"

"Car crash," I said plainly.

"Geez, Vanessa, I'm so sorry."

I had really begun to hate those words, even though I knew people only said them to be kind. I didn't deserve anyone's pity, but I couldn't exactly come right out and admit that. "It's okay." I lifted my cup to my lips and took a sip of coffee. "Enough about me. What about you? Are you married? Any kids?"

His expression darkened. "Not anymore. Kristi, that's my ex-wife, and I just signed the papers on the world's ugliest divorce a few weeks ago."

It was my turn to offer condolences. "Is that why you moved back down this way?"

He nodded. "I needed to get away. I never really liked living in Pollock Pines. There's nothing to do up there, and everyone knows your business. If it wasn't for my job and my family, I probably would've moved all the way to the east coast just to get away from everything." There was an unmistakable bitter tinge to his voice.

"That bad?"

"You have no idea."

"My friend Marla, the one that was with me at the gym the other day, she had a pretty rough divorce, too, a few years back. Apparently, her husband had a hard time keeping his you-know-what in his pants."

"Well, let's just put it this way. I know how she feels."

"Really?" Whoever his ex-wife was, I instantly hated her. If Kristi were to walk up to me right this second and tell me she volunteered at a homeless shelter every week, I'd tell her I didn't care. She'd cheated on Alex Brooks. That was enough to make me mark her down as heartless in my book.

"You seem surprised."

"It's hard for me to believe someone would actually cheat on a guy like you."

He arched one of his brows. "A guy like me?"

"You're such a nice guy," I said. The thing about Alex was that despite his good looks, he was also kind. And he wasn't just like that to his circle of friends, he was nice to everyone. Guys like that didn't come along too often. Unless he'd changed. "At least you were back in high school."

He cracked a smile. "Is that really the way you saw me?"

I nodded.

His smile faded. "You know what they say about nice guys, right?"

I frowned. "Your ex-wife is a fool."

Alex shifted in his seat. He wasn't any more comfortable talking about his failed marriage than I was talking about Ryan. "Let's talk about something else. Why don't you tell me about your kids?"

I smiled. Alex had no idea what he'd just gotten himself into. I could talk about Jacob and Lydia for days. I pulled out my phone to show him pictures. While I explained how Jacob was sensitive and bright and Lydia was affectionate and talented, Alex sat there, patiently listening like he was actually interested.

"They sound like great kids," he said. He took a sip of his coffee then shook his head.

He had something on the tip of his tongue. I could just feel it. "What is it? What are you thinking?"

"I can't believe Vanessa King is a mother. Not that I didn't think you would be, it's just I still remember you back in high school swearing you were never getting married or having kids. Yet here you are, a mother of two."

"It's Vanessa Collins now," I said. "And as you already know, a lot can change in twenty years."

"Yes, it can," Alex agreed. "Do you keep in touch with anyone else from our old high school?"

"A few people but mostly on Facebook." I pulled out my phone again and scrolled through my friends list showing Alex pictures of some of our former classmates. I pointed to a picture of a girl I knew he used to date. "Tanya's married to some cardiologist now, and they've got a giant house in the Fab Forties."

I'd often fantasized about living in the Fab Forties, a posh neighborhood in Midtown Sacramento where all the homes had perfectly manicured lawns and regularly sold for well over a million dollars.

"Doesn't surprise me," he said. "It's for the best. She wouldn't have been happy with a blue-collar guy like me."

I gave him a wry look. "Would you have been happy with someone as high maintenance as her?"

Alex smiled, and before he could stop himself, he started laughing. "You're right. Tanya and I were polar opposites. I still don't know why I agreed to go out with her."

"Wait. She was the one who asked you out?"

He nodded.

"Well, you probably just said yes because you didn't want to hurt her feelings," I said. "Or maybe it's because she's drop-dead gorgeous."

"It wasn't that. Believe it or not, some of us guys realize there's more to a person than the way they look."

My heart did that weird somersault thing again. Alex had always been different than a lot of other guys I knew. It was nice to hear that he hadn't changed.

He glanced down at his phone. "Oh shit," he said grabbing it and stuffing it in his back pocket. "I've got to be at work in fifteen minutes. Where the hell did the time go?"

We'd been at the coffee shop for almost an hour. I hadn't realized it had been that long either. Alex stood and pulled his jacket on. "Can we do this again sometime?" he asked. "Maybe next time we can grab some dinner?"

"Dinner? Um, okay. Sure."

"I'll text you later tonight." Alex turned to leave, almost stumbling over his chair. He glanced over his shoulder, sparing me a quick bashful look before darting out the door.

He'd taken off so quickly that I didn't quite realize I'd agreed to meet him again until I got into my car. It wouldn't be a date, I reminded myself as I turned the engine on. Just two old friends getting reacquainted. Having male friends again would be fun. When Ryan and I were together, he'd get upset if he even saw me having a conversation with another guy. He didn't believe men and women could be just friends.

As I pulled out of the parking lot, something dawned on me. Alex had managed to make me smile in a way I hadn't for a long time. It didn't mean anything, though. That was just the kind of thing that happened when you ran into a friend you hadn't seen in forever and reminisced about old times. I wasn't going to feel guilty about it. Even *I* deserved to smile every now and then.

9

"It wasn't a date," I told Marla *again* when she popped over with her kids after school a few days later.

"Then why'd he ask you out for dinner?"

"What he asked was if I wanted to grab dinner sometime, which isn't exactly the same thing as, 'hey, would you like to have dinner with me?'" I clarified. "He also said he'd text me, but he hasn't, so I'm sure he didn't mean anything by it."

"Let's just say, hypothetically, that Alex did ask you out on a date. What would you say?"

"I'd say no. Because I'm not dating him or anyone else ever again," I said, my voice dead serious so she'd know I meant it.

Marla's eyes widened. Clearly, she hadn't expected that response, though I had no idea why. She, more than anyone, knew what I'd been through with Ryan.

"You have to at least give dating a chance."

I shook my head. "No, I don't. Love is a lie. I learned that from Ryan the hard way. It all starts out the same way. With sweet words and gifts, and then after they snare you, the truth comes out."

I was convinced that was the reason Ryan had proposed so

soon after we started dating. He was afraid that once I saw what he was really like, I'd bail. But I'd gotten so swept up in the romance, the conviction in love at first sight, and Ryan being my one true love that I didn't stop to ponder why he wanted things between us to move so swiftly.

Marla tilted her head to the side just a little. "Not all guys are like that."

"You're right. But I don't know how to sniff out the nice guys from the jerks, so I'll just leave the dating to the women who do. I'm fine on my own, and so are the kids."

Marla sighed and got up to help herself to a glass of water. I could tell she had more to say, but thankfully, she kept it to herself. If Alex ever did text or call, I'd agree to meet with him again, as friends only. And if he ever expressed a desire for more, I'd politely tell him I wasn't interested. I had two kids to raise, on my own. With their school stuff and soccer and Lydia's gymnastics, I was drowning in activities. Jacob kept bugging me about joining band, and no matter how much I wanted to say no, I knew I wouldn't. My kids were down one parent, and I planned on making up for it any way I knew how, even if that meant enduring trumpet practice and cringe-worthy band performances.

BY THE FOLLOWING WEEK, I was sure Alex had forgotten all about the dinner he'd mentioned. I shrugged it off. It was better not to let him get too close. I remembered the funny little backflip my heart had done the last time I'd seen him. I didn't need him confusing my already-confused life.

I'd almost completely pushed all thoughts of him out of my mind when I ran into him a few days later at the grocery store, of all places. I'd just put a bag of organic tortilla chips into my shopping cart when I heard his voice behind me.

"Just because they're organic doesn't mean they're any better for you," he teased.

I turned my head and smiled. "Great, now what am I going to snack on, you party pooper?"

He returned my smile and reached into his shopping cart. "Personally, I like these," he said, holding up a box of ice cream sandwiches.

"You're not going to try and convince me those are healthy, are you?"

"Well, they've got calcium—"

"And more fat and calories than I should be eating in a day."

His smile faded. "You've got a good point there."

"So how have you been?" I asked.

"Good. Just been busy putting in lots of extra hours at work."

Was that why he hadn't texted? Not that it mattered. I'd put more stock into his on-the-fly dinner invitation than I should have.

"I'm off for the next three days though," he said. "Maybe we can grab some dinner tonight?"

I hesitated before replying, "Tonight's not good." As much fun as having dinner with Alex sounded, I just couldn't. "I'm a single mom now, and my kids aren't old enough for me to leave them home by themselves." I supposed I could ask Marla, but then she'd just give me the third degree after, and I wasn't up for another discussion about my love life.

"Right. I hadn't thought about that." He rubbed his right temple with his fingertips. "Maybe you can bring them. We can get some pizza. Kids love pizza."

"How would you know that?" He hadn't mentioned having kids when I'd asked him.

"All kids love pizza. That's just common knowledge."

I was almost tempted to say yes, but something stopped me. I didn't want to confuse Jacob and Lydia. Hanging out with Alex would be fun. Even though I worked full-time, most of my job duties got done at home, which meant I didn't get a lot of opportunities to interact with people my own age. Sometimes I missed it. But my children came first.

"I don't know. They're kind of ... shy."

"Well, how about coffee again sometime instead?"

I shrugged. "Sure. Just let me know when."

"Can we do it tomorrow?"

I hadn't expected such an eager response. "Okay," I said. "Same place and time as last time?"

"Works for me."

"I'll see you then," I said then turned and headed down the grocery store aisle.

For some strange reason, running into Alex had lifted my mood, and I managed to sail through the rest of the morning, despite a conference call that almost put me to sleep. Then I went to pick up the kids. One look at Jacob's puffy eyes and tearstained cheeks and my heart completely deflated.

"What happened?" I asked as he slammed the car door shut.

"PE," he said lowering his head.

"What about PE?"

"I got picked last for teams again, and then Ash hit me in my shin with a hockey stick. On purpose!"

"Did you tell your PE teacher?"

Lydia groaned. "Mr. Maloney doesn't do anything."

"Ash just told him it was an accident," Jacob said.

Whoever that Ash kid was, I felt like punching him in his face. Despite being on a soccer team for the last three years, Jacob had never been the sportiest kid, and sometimes he got teased about it. Physical education, or PE as the kids called it, was quickly becoming his least favorite subject in school.

"Let's just forget about PE and that stupid Ash kid," I said. "Why don't we go and get some frozen yogurt?"

"Frozen yogurt. Yay!" Lydia lifted her arms in the air, excited, while Jacob just mumbled a barely audible "okay."

Thankfully, by the time Jacob finished topping his frozen yogurt with gummy bears, sprinkles, and whipped cream, a smile finally appeared on his handsome face. It felt good to know that I'd put it there. Sometimes the small victories were the most satisfying. I hadn't been wrong when I'd told Marla I didn't plan on dating ever again. My kids came first. It was just the three of us now, and I kind of liked it that way.

When Ryan was alive, I felt like I constantly had to protect our children from his temper. Ryan sometimes said things to them, hurtful things. Things that I know stayed with them. As I watched Jacob and Lydia eat their frozen yogurt, I thought back to a few weeks before Ryan's accident. I'd come home from the gym on a Sunday to find Ryan hovering over Jacob, who was cowering in the corner of the living room. Tears streamed down my son's face.

"What's going on here?" I asked.

Ryan turned his head in my direction. "What's going on is your son almost broke his sister's fingers."

"How did that happen?"

"He slammed the door on my hand." I glanced at Lydia, who stood a few feet away, her face pale. "But I told Daddy it was just an accident."

Ryan smacked Jacob.

The sound of his hand making contact with my son's cheek, followed by Jacob crying out, set my insides on fire. I ran across the room, putting myself between Jacob and his father. "Leave him alone!"

"You're always defending him. He doesn't need a mama bear. He needs discipline."

"Lydia said it was an accident."

Ryan glared at me. Without another word, he stormed away, down the hall and into the bedroom, slamming the door behind himself. That's when Jacob broke down crying. I pulled him into my arms, sick to my stomach. I'd made the choice to marry Ryan, to have children with him. Children that I sometimes had to protect from their very own father. I hated it, and I hated how helpless I felt.

But the thing was Ryan wasn't always bad with them. Sometimes he doted on them more than I did. It made deciding what was right impossibly hard. Just when Ryan would push me far enough that I swore a divorce was my only option, he'd change. Ryan would soften. He'd start helping around the house. He'd play with the kids. More than once, after Jacob had heard us arguing, he told me he didn't want us to get divorced. Despite everything his father did, he still loved him. Kids were forgiving that way.

I wondered if Jacob's tears from earlier weren't just about some mean kid in his class and being picked last for PE. Maybe they were the tears of a nine-year-old who missed his father. I was the kind of mother who liked to fix things for her kids, but I couldn't fix Ryan's death for them. The thought almost made *me* feel like crying.

Instead, I smiled at my children and ruffled Jacob's hair first then his sister's.

"You guys know how much I love you, right?"

They smiled and replied in chorus, "Yeah. We do."

10

I woke up the next day to a gray drizzly morning. It was almost April. The sun was supposed to be out. It never snowed in Sacramento, but the winters were chilly and rainy. Once spring hit, it stayed sunny and warm for extended periods of time, but sometimes there were late-in-the-season storms. This was apparently one of those days. The bad weather put me in such a funk, I almost texted Alex to cancel our coffee plans. I didn't even want to spend time with me, so why would Alex? I hated the idea of bailing on him last minute though, so after dropping the kids off at school, I drove over to the coffee shop where we'd met last time.

As soon as I stepped inside, Alex waved. I walked over to him. "I already got you a mocha," he said. "Figured you'd want the same drink you got last time."

"Thanks." I took a seat and managed a smile, trying to cover my murky mood.

"You look nice," he said.

I ran a hand through my hair, still moist from the drizzle outside. "Thank you," I said, even though I had a hard time believing he really meant it. I felt like a hot mess, which in my mind, meant that I looked like one too. Alex, on the other hand, really did look amazing. I suddenly wondered if he was dating anyone. I was about to ask him, when it dawned on me that if he wasn't, he probably would be soon. Guys like him didn't stay single long. "You do too."

"I was wondering something the other day when I ran into you at the grocery store."

"Oh yeah?" I asked. "And what would that be?"

Alex took a sip of his coffee before continuing. "How come I haven't seen you at the gym again? What time do you usually go?"

"To be honest, I haven't been going very often. Not since Ryan died. Between work and trying to deal with all his final arrangements, life's been so busy. Not to mention all the cooking and cleaning and housework. Why do you ask?"

"Any chance I can convince you to start going again?"

I frowned. "Why? Are you trying to hint at something?"

It took a moment for Alex to get what I was saying. His eyes widened. "Oh no, not at all. I mean, you look great, perfect in fact. I just ... I need someone to keep me motivated. I was going to ask if you wanted to go together. We could be workout buddies."

"Workout buddies?" I mulled his words over in my mind. I usually worked out alone. Every now and then, I went to the gym with Marla but not very often. When we did go together, working out was always more fun. The more I thought about it, the more I liked the idea. If I had someone to exercise with, maybe it wouldn't be so hard for me to finally get back into my old fitness routine. And I'd get to see Alex more often, an idea I liked more than I should have. I didn't want to seem too eager, though. "Hmm, I don't know."

"C'mon," he urged. When I didn't give him an answer, he continued. "Just so you know, I'm not above begging."

How could I say no? Especially when my heart was doing that annoying thump-thump thing again. "Okay," I said then took a sip of my coffee, trying to come across as casual. "You got yourself a deal."

He smiled, and I swore my heart stopped beating for a moment. Years ago, he'd had that same effect on me, but I was way too shy to tell him back then. There were so many girls vying for his attention that I didn't think I stood a chance. We'd kissed once, on a dare at a party, and sitting there across the table from him, the memory flashed in my mind, more vivid than it should have been considering how long ago it had happened.

I pushed the image out of my head and searched for something to talk about. Anything to get me to stop imagining what Alex looked like shirtless and sweaty after a workout. "So besides going to the gym and working, how else do you spend your time?" I wondered what being both single and childless was like. It had been so many years since I'd been both of those that I hardly remembered it.

Alex shrugged. "I sleep a lot and watch way more Netflix than I should."

He sounded a little sad. For a moment, I was tempted to reach for his hand. It's what I would have done when we'd been friends all those years ago. I had to remind myself that plenty had changed since then. "I'm sure soon enough you'll find your real Miss Right, and before you know it, you'll have a house full of children. And then you'll *never* get to watch Netflix again, no matter how bad you really want to."

He shook his head. "I doubt it. I don't even think I can have children."

I frowned. "Why do you say that?"

"I was married for twelve years, Vanessa, and it never happened."

Twelve years? Wow, he'd gotten married young. I had no idea why that surprised me so much, but it did. "Maybe it was your ex's fault."

"Nope. It definitely wasn't. Kristi can have kids."

I wondered how he knew that. Maybe she'd already moved on with someone else and had a baby with her new guy. That was probably why Alex sounded so bitter. I'd feel the same way if I were in his shoes. Love really sucked sometimes.

"I'm sorry. I didn't mean to bring up painful memories."

"You have nothing to be sorry for. I mean, sure, going through a divorce is shitty, but it can't be worse than what you're going through. I can't even imagine losing someone I love the way you did."

I took a deep breath. "I don't know. Maybe divorce is worse. Especially when it's long and drawn out and the person you're getting divorced from hurt you and betrayed you," I said. In some ways, divorce seemed a lot like death, except instead of losing the person you cared about suddenly, you lost them slowly, bit by bit over days, weeks, and months. Sure, their physical body was still around, but who they once were was gone. "Don't get me wrong, getting that call from the emergency room about Ryan's car crash was hard. But the truth is, we didn't have that great a marriage, so I still don't really know what to feel about him being gone." I couldn't believe I'd just confessed that, but I felt like I had to. I didn't want him getting the wrong idea that I was some grieving widow who'd lost her one true love, because it wasn't like that at all. Maybe he'd think I was a bad person, but I believed in honesty.

"You mean he wasn't the love of your life?" Alex sounded genuinely surprised.

"No." I shook my head. If someone had asked me that question ten years ago, I would've answered differently. Back then, I had all sorts of silly romantic notions, but now I didn't think I even believed in that kind of love anymore. "Why? Was Kristi yours?"

"No," he said decisively. "She wasn't."

I had a sudden overwhelming desire to make things right for Alex. Not that I knew how, and even if I did, it was a bad idea. That was what I'd hoped to do with Ryan, but I'd failed miserably. I seemed to attract broken people and then set myself to the task of fixing them.

When Ryan and I had first met, I remembered thinking I'd never known anyone who seemed as lonely as he did. I wanted to save him from that sadness. When he talked about his family, I could relate because my situation wasn't all that different from his.

He hadn't grown up in Sacramento. Instead, he'd come here for college, but he wasn't really sure what he'd wanted to study, which was why it took him until he was twenty-five to graduate. In the seven years he'd been in Sacramento before we'd met, he'd only made a handful of friends, and they weren't close ones. That should've been a huge red flag for me, but instead, I decided it was everyone else's fault. He would've had more friends if people had given him a chance. Back then, I was so smitten with Ryan that I hadn't realized the truth. His temper drove people away. It was always the same scenario. Ryan would become friends with someone. He'd invite them over to dinner. They'd hang out for a while, and then something would get Ryan upset, and he'd speak his mind and say things that made me gasp even though I'd seen the same situation play out time and time again. Ryan seemed to have no idea that words mattered. That you couldn't just say whatever you felt like without consequences.

I wound up being the one that filled the empty space in Ryan's life. Because of me, he wasn't alone anymore. I'd saved him, and I liked that. It made me feel important, like I was his own personal hero. Over time, I realized the notion of saving someone was completely foolish.

"Not to change the conversation too drastically," Alex said, pulling me out of my thoughts, "but, um, when do you think we'll be able to start this workout partner thing?"

"Give me another week. I need to arrange a few things with my work schedule."

"Okay, that sounds good." Alex reached around the back of his chair for his jacket. "I better get going, but I'll see you next week. Right? Eight thirty. At the gym. I'm holding you to it."

I smiled. "Yeah. I'll be there."

I watched as Alex walked out the door and over to his car, a gunmetal-gray Honda SUV.

Workout buddies? What had I just agreed to? I didn't like the way my body responded to him every time I was in his presence. That didn't bode well for me.

MARLA CAME over for dinner later that evening. I hadn't planned on telling her about agreeing to be Alex's workout buddy, but since we did go to the gym together occasionally, I figured that eventually she'd find out, so I shared the news over spaghetti and salad.

"Workout buddies?" She gave me a quizzical look. "Doesn't that mean you two will be seeing each other quite a bit."

I knew what she was hinting at.

"As friends," I reminded her. "Nothing more."

"Who's Alex?" Lydia asked.

"Just an old friend from high school that I ran into a few weeks ago."

"Is Alex a girl or boy?" Jacob asked.

"Alex is a he," I replied.

"Oooh, Mommy's got a boyfriend," Lydia said in a singsongy voice.

"He is not my boyfriend," I said, making sure to keep my voice soft so Marla wouldn't accuse me of protesting too much.

"He's a boy, and he's your friend," Jacob said. "So, technically, he is your boyfriend."

I glanced at Marla. "A little help here."

"You're on your own," she said before lifting a forkful of pasta into her mouth.

"Let's talk about something else," I said.

"Great idea," Marla agreed, finally coming to my aid. "Guess where Caleb is having his birthday party?" Caleb was one of Marla's three kids. The middle child. His older sister was Abby, and his little brother was Caden.

"Bounce High?" Lydia asked, eagerly. She couldn't get enough of bounce houses. Bounce High was where she'd had her last two birthday parties.

"Nope, he's going to have a bowling party."

Lydia frowned. "I don't know how to bowl."

"It's super easy. I can teach you." Marla reached into her purse and pulled out an invitation.

Thankfully, talking about Caleb's upcoming birthday party was enough to stop all discussion of Mommy having a boyfriend.

As Marla chatted with Jacob and Lydia about the special shoes you got for bowling, I sat there, imagining what my kids would think if I really did start dating. Neither Jacob nor Lydia seemed upset about the idea, but that's because they'd just been joking around about it. It would probably be a different story if I really did meet someone. Not that I wanted to or ever planned on it.

Still, I couldn't help but wonder.

11

It had been almost three months since Ryan died, and I kept waiting for Jacob or Lydia to show me or tell me something that would clue me in about how they felt about their dad being gone. I'd begun to think that maybe they were just exceptionally good at adjusting to their new reality. Then one night, I woke up to the sound of a bloodcurdling scream coming from Lydia's room. I jumped out of bed and ran down to her room. I flicked on the light switch to find her sitting up in bed, tears streaming down her face.

"What happened? Did you have a bad dream?" I asked, wrapping my arms around her.

She was crying so hard she couldn't even speak. Instead, she just nodded her little head.

"Can you tell me what it was about?"

It took her a few minutes to calm down enough to get words out. "It was about Daddy and the car crash," she managed to say. "I was in the car with him, and there were bad guys chasing us, and that's why Daddy crashed the car."

"Oh, honey. I'm so sorry." I let go of her and wiped her tearstained cheeks with my fingertips. "I know you miss your daddy and that you're scared because he isn't here anymore, but I promise you there are no bad guys. What happened to your father, it was an accident."

"I ... I know," she said as another round of tears streamed down her cheeks. "But it was so real."

"Listen to me." I waited for her to look into my eyes. "Mommy would never let anything bad happen to you. You believe me, right?"

Lydia nodded. I kissed the top of her head and hugged her again, maybe just a little bit too tightly, but I couldn't help it. She was my little girl, my baby, despite being almost seven. For a few minutes, we just sat there. I stroked her hair until I felt the fear leaving her little body.

"You think you're ready to try and go back to sleep?" I asked, my voice soft.

She looked up and stared at me with sad eyes still red from crying. "Can I sleep next to you?"

How could I say no? "Okay." I smiled at her then scooped her into my arms and carried her down the hallway and into my bedroom. Once she was under the covers, I turned the light off.

"Mommy," she said a few minutes after settling in beside me.

"What is it, honey?"

"I miss Daddy."

I hugged her tighter. "I know you do. I'm so sorry that he's not with us anymore, sweetness."

"I'll always have you, though, right?"

"Of course you will," I said, kissing her soft little cheek.

Lydia let out a deep sigh. My room never got completely dark because of the light that streamed in from the streetlamps outside. I waited for my little girl to close her eyes. Then I watched her chest rise and fall with each breath she took. God, I loved my kids so much. I often wondered if other parents felt the same way I did. Ryan resented how much I doted on Jacob and

Lydia because it took attention away from him. He'd get mad over stupid stuff like whenever I made the kids' favorite dinner instead of his.

"You're a grown-up," I used to tell him. "If you don't like what I made, you can always cook something else for yourself. The kids can't."

Sometimes he felt like a third child instead of a husband. He exhausted me with his endless demands. When we were newly-weds and before we had kids, I did my best to meet every single one of them, but eventually I realized I'd never succeed. No matter how hard I tried, Ryan would complain that I didn't truly love him, that I probably didn't want to be married to him, that I was interested in someone else. He had an endless list of complaints. One day it hit me. Ryan was perennially dissatisfied. Nothing would ever be enough for him.

I hoped Lydia's nightmare would be a one-time thing, but a few nights later, she had another one and then again a few days after that. It took twice as long to calm her down.

"Honey, you've got school in the morning. You've got to go back to sleep."

"But I can't sleep without you."

So I brought her into bed with me again.

I woke up the next morning feeling like a zombie and prayed that this didn't become a regular thing. I didn't do well with less than six hours of sleep. I still vividly remembered when the kids were younger and would sometimes get high fevers or throw up when they got sick. I'd be up all night worrying and stuffing load after load of vomit-covered sheets into the washing machine. It was dreadful. Now that they were older, it was nice getting to sleep through the night. I did not want to go back to those days.

Despite being wickedly tired, I dropped the kids off at school and headed to the gym. After leaving my purse in the locker room, I searched for Alex and found him in the cardio room.

"You're going to have to take it easy on me today," I told him. "I've had less than six hours of sleep."

His eyes filled with concern. "Why, what happened?"

I explained about Lydia's nightmares.

"Has she been having them ever since your husband died?"

I shook my head and then hopped onto a stationary bike, the only machine I could manage given my combination of sleep deprivation and poor fitness after skipping the gym for so many months. "No, for some strange reason, they just started. But this is the third one she's had over the past week. I'm not really sure what to do."

Alex took the bike beside me. "Maybe what she needs is some one-on-one time with you," he suggested.

In theory, it was a great idea. I wondered why I hadn't thought of it on my own. The one problem with Alex's suggestion was who would watch Jacob? I supposed I could ask Marla or Lynette, but then Jacob would wonder what I was up to with Lydia. If I spent one-on-one time with Lydia, I'd have to do the same for Jacob. That was only fair. I didn't explain that to Alex, though. He didn't have children of his own, so I doubted he'd understand. Instead, I gave him a weak smile. "I'm sure it's just a temporary thing," I said, hoping I was right. If I wasn't, then I really would have to give Alex's suggestion some serious consideration.

"You think you're up for some weight training?" Alex asked after we pedaled in silence for a few minutes.

"Yeah," I replied, breathless from pedaling.

"Five more minutes of warm-up, and then let's go do some arms."

I followed Alex's lead. He seemed to know a lot more about fitness than I did. I took turns with him on the bicep machine, trying not to notice how amazingly well sculpted his arms were.

I couldn't help but imagine what the rest of him looked like under his T-shirt and shorts.

We moved on to a machine I'd never used before. The sticker pasted to it read: *Lat Pulldown*. Whatever that was. Despite Alex's demonstration, I could tell I was not doing it right. He placed his hand on the small of my back, helping me with my posture. The weird thumping thing my heart sometimes did around him returned. I glanced at him out of the corner of my eye, wondering if he felt what I was feeling and if I could find the answer in his expression.

The only thing I saw was his intent focus on making sure I had the right form. "I don't want you to get injured," he said.

Right. I didn't want that either. I reminded myself again that we were just friends. I hadn't had a platonic relationship with a man in so long that I forgot how things were supposed to work. I wasn't supposed to be lusting after him. I wondered what Alex would say if I asked him for some benefits to go along with our friendship. Not that I ever would. I'd never been a one-night-stand or sex-without-commitment type of woman. Still, I couldn't help but wonder if he'd take me up on the offer.

I managed to make it through the rest of our workout session without letting my mind travel to places it had no business going. When we were finished, I grabbed my purse from the locker I'd stashed it in and met Alex in the small lounge area near the entrance to the gym.

"You all right?" he asked. "I didn't work you out too hard, did I?"

"No. I'm good."

"C'mon," he said, holding the door open for me. "Let me walk you to your car."

I followed him outside. In the hour since I'd arrived at the gym, it had warmed up nicely. Sacramento was one of those places where you used the heater in the morning and the air conditioning at night. Well into the summer, mornings could be downright chilly even on days when temperatures soared into the eighties later.

"Are we still on for tomorrow?" he asked as I pulled my car keys out of my purse.

"I think so." I opened the door. "Depends on how sore I am."

"We'll work on legs tomorrow so your arms can rest."

"Well, in that case, I wouldn't want to miss it," I said sarcastically.

"Just consider it a favor for an old friend," Alex said with a heart-melting grin. "If it wasn't for you, I'd have walked out of the gym halfway through today's workout."

"Yeah, I'm a regular Jillian Michaels," I said, referring to the hard-core trainer on some reality show I used to watch every now and then. Alex just smiled again. I got into my car and pulled out of the parking lot, noticing that he stood there watching.

The next morning, I woke up sore just like I knew I would, but I powered through another workout session with Alex anyway. Not because I particularly felt like it, but because I wanted to see Alex again. By the end of the week, I'd decided there was nothing wrong with admiring him from afar. My imagination was about the only place I'd be getting it on with him, but it was safe there. Eventually, Alex would heal from his divorce, and then he'd find himself ready to date again. He would leave the safe harbor my friendship offered and venture into more adventurous waters, but I was mature enough to deal with that when it happened. For now, I appreciated the way things were, and I decided to not think about the inevitable change that was bound to come.

This was the smoothest my life had been in a long time, and I planned on enjoying the ride for as long as I could.

12

A nother week went by. On Friday, after picking the kids up from school, I emptied out their backpacks just like I always did, sorting through their homework assignments, tests, and art projects from the week. Mixed up in all that stuff was a flyer that read: "Annual Father-Son Event."

I laid it down on the table, wondering if Jacob had seen it. He'd gone with his father every year since kindergarten. The event consisted of dodgeball in the school's gymnasium, accompanied by top-forty hits, junk food, and socializing. Tickets to the event sold out every year. By Monday, there'd be posters all over the school grounds, promoting it, if they weren't already up. Even if I threw the flyer in the trash, there was no way Jacob wouldn't realize that it was that time of year. How would he feel when his buddies talked about it at recess and he had nothing to add to the conversation?

I decided to find out. I headed down the hallway and knocked on his bedroom door. "Can I come in?"

He was lying on his bed, watching YouTube videos on his tablet. "Yeah," he said, sitting up.

I took a seat beside him and handed him the flyer. "How do you feel about this?"

Jacob just shrugged and laid the flyer on the bed beside him. "I don't feel anything about it."

"You went with your father every year—"

"Because he made me. I never even wanted to go."

That came as a surprise to me. I frowned. "Why didn't you ever say anything?"

"Because you know how Daddy was. I didn't want him to get mad at me, so I just went. And besides, they had Doritos, so it was okay."

"You're saying you only went so Daddy wouldn't get mad?"

He nodded. "And for the Doritos."

I knew Jacob was trying to be funny by mentioning the Doritos, but I couldn't bring myself to laugh. I hated that he'd felt forced into doing something he didn't want to just to keep his father from getting upset.

"I wish you would've said something." Jacob looked up at me without responding, his eyes blinking every few seconds just like they always did when he felt uneasy about something. "Can you talk to me about how you're feeling about your father being gone? I know you don't really like discussing your feelings, but I need to know if you're okay or not."

"I'm okay," he said, lowering his eyes and staring at his hands folded in his lap. "I mean, I'm sad Daddy is dead, and I do miss him sometimes, but ..."

"But what?" I asked.

"You're going to think I'm a bad person."

"No, I won't," I insisted, reaching for his hand.

"Sometimes I'm glad he's gone," Jacob said, his voice barely above a whisper. "I feel like life is easier when he's not around."

"And you're ashamed for thinking that way?"

His expression gave him away. He nodded slowly. "I told you I'm a bad person."

"You are *not* a bad person." I pulled him into my arms. "You're a human person and one of the kindest, sweetest ones I've ever known."

He started crying. His tears soaked into my shirt. "I can't stop thinking that I'm bad."

I dropped my arms from around him, leaned back, and wrapped my hands around his wrists, staring into his tear-filled eyes. "Daddy wasn't nice all the time. Sometimes he could be downright mean. There's nothing wrong with not missing someone who's hurt you."

"But sometimes he could be nice too."

"And when you remember those times, you miss him, don't you?"

He nodded.

"And when you think about the times he got angry, you don't?"

He nodded again.

"That's perfectly normal, Jakey. It doesn't mean you're bad."

I thought back to when my dad had left. I was so young that I didn't have many memories of him, so I didn't really miss him. I missed the idea of a father but not the actual person who had been my dad.

I smoothed Jacob's hair to the side. It was getting so long that it almost reached his eyes. I needed to find the time to take him for a haircut. "You're not bad," I told him again. "As a matter of fact, you're one of the nicest boys I've ever met."

"You're just saying that because you're my mom."

"Nope. I'd say it no matter whose son you were." I managed to get a hint of a smile out of Jacob. "So you're sure you're okay missing this father-son thing?" I asked.

"Yeah. It's not actually that much fun. I don't really like

dodgeball. And they turn up the music so loud that it gives me a headache."

It was a relief to know that he wasn't interested in going, and I was glad that Jacob and I had this talk and that he'd trusted me enough to let me know what was going on in his head. "You know I love you, right?"

He nodded and reached for his tablet. I took it from him. "How about instead of YouTube we find a movie we can all watch together?" I didn't like how much time he spent alone in his room.

"Do I get to pick the movie?"

I nodded.

"Will you make some popcorn?"

"What are you, some kind of expert negotiator?"

"What does that mean?"

I smiled. "Nothing. Of course I'll make us some popcorn." I stood then pulled him to his feet.

Lydia was on the couch, watching TV. She wasn't happy about her show being interrupted, nor was she thrilled with her brother's choice of movie. She was still deep into her princess phase and wanted to watch *Frozen* for the thousandth time, but I explained that I'd promised Jacob he could pick the movie. "You get to choose next time."

At bedtime, as I tucked the kids in, Jacob insisted once more that he was okay, but I couldn't help but worry. I struggled with guilt on an almost-daily basis, but I was an adult. I could handle it. I wasn't so sure that a nine-year-old could. I thought of Marla's offer to give me the name of the therapist she'd taken her kids to after her divorce and considered calling her to ask for his number. I just wasn't sure how comfortable my kids would be talking to a stranger about their feelings.

People said that once you got past the baby phase, parenthood got easier. I didn't agree. When my kids were babies, parenting was definitely less complicated. They had fairly basic needs: food, baths, diaper changes. Things got more difficult when one of them got sick or their teeth started coming in, but back then, parenting had been pretty straightforward. The older my kids got, the trickier things got. Just sticking a milk-filled breast into their mouth to soothe them was no longer an option. Sometimes it was so difficult to know what to do. No matter how much I loved it, being a mother was a lot harder than I'd ever imagined.

By Monday morning, I still hadn't stopped worrying about Jacob. I found myself thinking about him while I warmed up on the elliptical machine, hoping that he'd meant it when he'd told me he really didn't want to go to the father-son event and that he hadn't just said what he thought I'd wanted to hear.

"You're really quiet today," Alex said as we headed to the weight room. "Is everything all right?"

The words came out before I could stop myself. I didn't want to dump my parenting worries on Alex, but I couldn't help myself. Sometimes, I just needed to talk about the jumbled-up mess of thoughts running around in my head. "I'm just worried about Jacob."

"Why? What happened?"

I started by telling Alex about the father-son-event flyer I'd fished out of Jacob's backpack.

He interrupted before I finished. "Maybe I could take him. I know we haven't met yet, but—"

"You're sweet to offer," I said, surprised but not really sure why I was. That was Alex's way. He'd always had a generous personality. "But it's not necessary. Jacob doesn't really want to go. Apparently, he never did, but he was too scared to tell his father."

"Oh?"

"Ryan could be emotionally manipulative at times. He wasn't the type of person you said no to. Not without consequences."

I could picture his response to Jacob telling him he didn't want to go to the father-son event. He'd probably say, "You just don't want to go because you don't love your father." Or something equally hurtful. And Jacob liked to avoid conflict at all costs.

"No offense, but Ryan sounds like a jerk."

I shrugged. "Sometimes he was."

"I don't want you to take this the wrong way," Alex said, "but I gotta ask. If things between you and Ryan were as bad as you make them sound, why were you still together? Why didn't you tell him you wanted a divorce?"

It was a question I'd asked myself a thousand times. Why didn't I just leave? For the past few years, I'd been downright miserable, and with each fight, things between us just got worse and worse. Half the time I could barely stand to be in the same room with Ryan. "We had two kids together. I've seen the way divorce upends children's lives. I didn't want to do that to them," I said, leaving out the part about being downright petrified. Not just of how Ryan would react, but of such a drastic life change. I hated the idea of only having my kids half the time. "And a part of me still kind of hoped that things would get better."

I wasn't really sure why. For years, I'd been trying to convince Ryan to go to marriage counseling, but he'd adamantly refused. Marla once told me I should threaten to leave him if he didn't agree to go, but I couldn't bring myself to do that. Not only was I scared of how he'd respond to an ultimatum like that, but no matter how many things Ryan said or did to hurt me, I couldn't bring myself to hurt him back, at least not purposefully. I endlessly fooled myself into thinking Ryan could change. After an especially big fight, he'd cool down. Sometimes he'd even apologize. He'd start helping out more and be kinder. Until something set him off again. It was a terrible way to live, but I was determined to endure. When the kids were babies, Ryan was tender with them, but as they got older, he started taking his anger out on them. That's when I began to question how much more I could take. Ryan pushed and pushed and pushed. Before he died, I'd been teetering on the edge, but I hadn't quite fallen off.

"I'm glad I never met the guy," Alex muttered. "Because I think if I had, I'd have punched him in his face."

"And why is that?"

His jaw twitched. "You don't deserve to be treated like that."

His concern touched me. I hadn't even told him the half of it, but I understood his feelings. That was my exact thought when Alex had told me about his cheating ex-wife. I wanted to throttle her for hurting him.

I smiled and shook my head. "You haven't changed at all. You're still such a sweet guy."

"I mean it." He turned his head and stared at me, his blue eyes suddenly stormy. "If you were my wife, I'd make a point of showing you how special you are. Every. Single. Day."

My toes practically curled. It wasn't just his words but the look on his face. Maybe I wasn't the only one of us fantasizing that we were more than friends. Just for a moment, I imagined what it would be like to be married to him. I wondered how his lips felt, and his touch. I pictured myself wrapped in his strong but gentle arms before bed each night. It seemed so peaceful and the total opposite of how things had been with Ryan. I'd been a different person when Ryan and I first met. Back then I'd been drawn to the drama. Ryan's jealousy meant he loved me. His mood swings meant he was sensitive and broody. Somewhere along the way, I'd changed. Maybe it was because of the kids, or maybe I'd just grown up. Maybe that was one of the reasons Ryan had been so angry with me all the time. I'd changed, and he didn't like the new me.

I tried to push those thoughts out of my head. It didn't make sense for me to obsess over the past. Just like it didn't make sense for me to imagine myself with Alex. When he was ready to date, it wouldn't be with a mother of two, it would be with someone young and sexy who could go out to dinner with him on a moment's notice instead of with someone who had to line up a babysitter. And even if he were interested, dating him would put our friendship at risk, which I didn't want to do. It was the best thing that had happened to me in a long time.

13

As the weeks marched on and the weather started to warm, I began to wonder what I'd do in the summer when the kids were out of school. Their last day was in a few more weeks, and while I loved the idea of sleeping later in the morning, finding a way to keep them busy so I could get work done was a challenge I faced every summer. Normally, they went to camp for a few weeks, but this year I wouldn't be able to afford that. Despite Ryan's life insurance payout, I had to be careful how I spent my money. If I didn't budget wisely, I'd run out.

I also wondered what I'd do about Alex and our morning workouts. I did not want to give them up. Being around Alex was almost intoxicating. Every time he helped me with my posture or put his hands on me to help me with an exercise, I felt a jolt of electricity run through me at the contact. And lately, I'd begun to wonder if he felt it too. Sometimes he'd get this far-off look in his eyes like he was fantasizing about me the way I fantasized about him. And sometimes he looked like he was drinking me in with his gaze. It was enough to set my insides on fire.

I could bring the kids to the gym with me and drop them off

at the Kids Club, but once they saw Alex and me together, they'd start asking questions. I didn't have anything to hide, but the kids would be curious about why I was spending so much time with a guy.

I wondered if Alex would think it was strange, me making a big deal out of him meeting my children even though we were just friends. But we spent enough time around each other that introducing him to my kids seemed like the logical thing to do.

"I know this is going to sound weird," I said, finally working up the courage to bring it up while we jogged beside each other on treadmills. "But how would you feel about coming over for dinner this Friday evening?"

He stumbled, and for a moment I thought he was going to fall off his machine. I could feel my face heat. Did he think I'd just asked him out on a date, and was he wondering how to let me down gently? That would be beyond embarrassing. And it would mean I'd been reading his signals all wrong. "To your house?"

"Yeah," I said. "The kids will be out of school soon, and if you still want to work out in the mornings, I'll have to bring them to the Kids Club," I quickly explained. "They're bound to see us talking and want to know who you are. That's kids for you. They're curious about everything." I was totally babbling, but I couldn't bring myself to stop. "I know you're not really used to kids—you might not even like them—but mine are really sweet. I swear. By the end of summer they might even start calling you Uncle Alex, but only if you're okay with it."

"With you as their mother, of course they are."

My face heated again. "So that means you're okay with meeting them?"

"I'd love to." He slowed his pace and glanced at me. "And just so you know, I happen to really like children."

I had no idea why, but hearing him say that was a huge relief.

Maybe because, in my Alex fantasies, he loved my kids and they loved him right back. I was such a sappy idiot.

"I don't get off work until seven thirty though, so I probably won't be able to make it to your place until around eight. Is that too late?"

"No, that's fine." I'd give my kids a snack after school, and that would tide them over until he arrived.

Alex didn't have much to say after that. Which was unusual. We normally found loads to talk about. I wanted to ask him what was wrong, but at the same time, I wasn't sure I wanted to stir things up. Maybe it was better to leave some things unsaid.

As the silence continued, I thought about telling Alex to forget about my awkward dinner invitation. I could put our morning workouts on pause until summer break was over. It would give me enough time to get my head straight. I'd meant it when I told Marla I had no intention of dating again. Ten years of marriage to Ryan had been painful enough. I didn't want to go through the hurt of another failed relationship.

Yet as Alex walked me to my car after we were done working out, I couldn't bring myself to say any of those things. Instead, I asked, "Is everything all right? You seem awfully quiet today."

"There's something I need to tell you, but I'm scared when I do, it'll screw up our friendship, and I really don't want that."

My heart sank. No matter what it was, I had to know what he was thinking. "Just say it." We'd reached my car, and needing to do something with my hands, I dug in my purse for my keys.

"I like you, Vanessa. Not just as friends either." I lifted my head to look at Alex while he spoke. "I've liked you since high school, really. I don't think I've ever stopped."

My eyes widened, but I couldn't think of anything to say. I was too focused on the sparks going off inside me, like a Fourth of July fireworks display. For weeks, I'd noticed the way his eyes lingered over me, but I was sure it would never amount to anything. I didn't think Alex would actually say anything about the unspoken attraction we had for each other.

"Can you please say something?"

"I ... I wasn't expecting that."

"Well then you're definitely not going to expect this, but since I'm already on a roll, I might as well just get it over with." Alex took a deep breath. "I want to meet your kids, but I don't want to be Uncle Alex. I want to be your boyfriend, and I want them to know that's what I am. Maybe not this Friday when I come over for the first time, that is if you still want me to. I mean somewhere down the road."

I stared at him, speechless again. This was not supposed to be happening. A thousand times I'd told myself I didn't want it to, but I'd been lying to myself. Still, I was content with my fantasies. Those were safe. The real thing was frightening. I quickly replayed the past few weeks in my head like a slideshow. Those times he touched my back or arms I half-assumed he was spotting me, but a part of me knew better, and I'd done nothing to discourage him. I'd told myself he wouldn't be attracted to a middle-aged widow with two kids and the less-than-perfect body that came with pregnancy and childbearing.

I wanted what he wanted, but I was too afraid to admit it. "What if I said no? Does that mean we can't be friends anymore?" The thought of not seeing him anymore made me feel ill, but so did the idea of getting hurt again. I'd never felt so conflicted.

He looked wounded. "No, of course not."

I shook my head and put my hands to my temples. "I'm no good at relationships, Alex. And I like the way things are now." God, what was I doing?

Alex stared at me for a moment, his eyes stormy. Then without another word, he turned around and walked away. I wanted to run after him and apologize. What was wrong with me? I wanted him. Why couldn't I just tell him that and give him a chance? Alex wasn't Ryan. With Ryan, I'd tumbled into a relationship before really getting to know him then an engagement and a marriage in about the same amount of time Alex and I had been working out together. Eighteen years might've passed, but Alex and I weren't strangers the way Ryan and I had been when we'd first met.

"Alex," I called out his name, half-expecting that he'd ignore me and keep walking. I'd just rejected him after all. Instead, he turned around and walked back over to me. He stared at me, his jaw hard and his eyes steel. I wanted to be his so badly.

"Listen. Just so you know, I'm not the kind of guy who can't take no for an answer," he said. The way he was looking at me made it feel like he could see through me, into my soul. "But this time is different. I just can't walk away. Not until I get you to see that we'd be great together."

"I ... I'm not good at relationships, Alex," I said again.

"That's only because you haven't been with the right man. I'm not some stranger you met at a bookstore. You and I, we have history. You know I'd never treat you the way your husband did. That's not who I am."

I did know that. So why was I still so scared? I looked into his eyes, resisting the urge to rest my hand on his cheek. "A lot of things have changed since high school."

"Not that many things."

"Alex, I—"

"You're scared," he said, somehow reading my mind. "But you don't have to be. I'd never hurt you."

He laced his fingers through mine. The feel of his skin on my skin was electric. My face heated, and my breath quickened. "Do you feel that?" he asked.

Holy shit. What was happening? With his other hand, he reached around the nape of my neck and pulled me closer.

Before I knew what was happening, he kissed me. Right in the middle of the gym parking lot. It only lasted a moment, but the taste of him, the feel of his lips on mine, was a million times better than it had been in my imagination.

He rested his forehead on mine, one hand still wrapped around the nape of my neck. He took a deep breath. "I'm sorry. I shouldn't have done that."

"It's okay." I rested my hand on his chest and felt his heart thumping under my palm. "I actually wanted you to."

"I hoped you did, but I wasn't sure. You're a hard woman to read, always have been."

"For the past few weeks, I've sort of been wondering what kissing you would feel like."

He smiled. "So? What did you think?"

"Better than I anticipated," I said, returning his smile.

"Does this mean what I think it does?"

I nodded. "But no rushing things. We have to take things slow. My kids come first, always. So that means on Friday, when you come over, no surprise kisses like the one you just gave me, no hand-holding, none of that. You have to let me tell Jacob and Lydia about us in my own time and in my own way."

"Us?" His grin melted my insides. "I like the sound of that."

"And you have to promise that no matter what happens, you'll be honest with me." It wasn't just my heart on the line but my kids' hearts too.

"I'd never lie to you. I swear."

"Okay, then it's official." I bit my lower lip to stop myself from smiling like an idiot. "We're dating." I could hardly believe it. How had we gone from zero to one hundred in a matter of minutes? Although the more I thought about it, the more I realized we hadn't. Not really. The signs were all there. I'd just chosen to pretend they weren't.

Alex put his hand on one of my cheeks and then leaned in to

kiss the other. When he pulled away, he licked his lips as if he were trying to taste me on them. My insides melted. "I can't wait until Friday."

I shook my head. This was crazy. I needed to get into my car quick before I turned into a giant puddle right in front of him. He stood there watching me drive away like he always did. And all I could think was what had I just gotten myself into?

14

That strange stomach-twisting, heart-racing feeling that comes when you first start falling for someone stayed with me all afternoon. I was both elated and frightened by it at the same time. The last person that had made me feel this way was Ryan, and that hadn't turned out very well. I reminded myself over and over again that I needed to keep a clear head. Alex and I hadn't even technically had a first date yet.

By three o'clock, when it was time to pick up Jacob and Lydia from school, I'd mentally rehearsed at least half a dozen times what I'd tell them about "Mommy's new friend." After we got home, I sat them down. "Before you guys start on your homework, there's something I want to talk to you about."

"What is it?" Lydia asked in her eager-little-girl way.

"I invited a friend over for dinner on Friday. Someone you two haven't met yet."

"I know who it is," Jacob said, grinning. "It's that guy Alex that you and Marla keep talking about."

I hadn't realized Marla and I talked about Alex that often. I was going to have to be more careful about not letting the kids overhear our conversations. "How did you know that?"

"I just guessed," Jacob said, sounding rather pleased with himself.

"If you don't want to meet him, just let me know. Okay?"

"Is he nice?" Lydia asked.

I smiled. "Very."

"Is he your boyfriend?"

Jacob elbowed his sister. "Didn't you hear Mommy? She said he's her friend."

"He is my friend. I've actually known him for a very long time. As a matter of fact, Alex and I went to high school together. But the truth is, I do like him. I like him a lot." As soon as the words were out of my mouth, I worried that I'd said too much.

"Wait, so he is your boyfriend?" Jacob asked.

I couldn't tell by his voice how he felt about the idea. "No. But I don't know. Maybe someday he might be. But that's only if you guys like him and think he's a nice guy."

Jacob and Lydia kind of glanced at each other like they were unsure of what to say or think. I wasn't sure what reaction I'd been expecting and worried that maybe I'd done the wrong thing by asking Alex over for dinner. Maybe it was just too soon. Their father had died only a few months ago.

"I think I'll like him," Lydia said.

"You like everybody," Jacob grumbled.

"I do not."

"Okay, guys, c'mon. This isn't something to fight about. I just wanted to let you know what's going on. That's all." Sometimes their sibling-rivalry thing drove me crazy.

"We're not fighting," Jacob insisted.

"I just want to make sure you guys are fine with me inviting Alex over."

"We're okay with it," Lydia and Jacob said together.

I was fairly certain Jacob and Lydia would more than like Alex. They had really big hearts, and since we had so little extended family to speak of, they tended to latch onto people quickly even though they were both kind of shy. But my biggest fear wasn't whether or not Jacob and Lydia would like Alex but that they'd like him too much, which meant, if things between Alex and me didn't work out, they'd be brokenhearted. Was I really up for taking such a huge chance? All morning, I'd been so giddy just thinking about the kiss Alex and I had shared in the gym parking lot, that I hadn't given enough thought to how having a boyfriend would affect my kids. Now I couldn't help but wonder if I was making a colossal mistake.

I wanted to believe in second chances. My relationship with Ryan had been an all-out disaster. Sometimes it felt like the only good thing that had come from meeting him were my children. But that didn't mean it would be that way with Alex. Like he'd said, he wasn't just some stranger I met in a bookstore. This time I knew what I was getting into. Or at least I prayed I did.

THE NEXT MORNING, after I arrived at the gym and found Alex waiting for me in our usual meet-up spot, the doubts that had plagued me all night slowly receded. One look at his face and those deep-blue eyes of his, and I thought back to that kiss in the parking lot and how good it had felt.

He greeted me with a smile. "I was getting worried you wouldn't show up."

"Sorry. I should have texted you. There was an accident on Fair Oaks, so it took me longer than normal to get here."

"That's okay." He gave me kiss on my forehead, and my insides melted. I hoped Alex didn't notice the blush I felt heating my face. "I don't want you texting and driving anyway."

"I gotta go put my bag in the locker. I'll find you in the cardio room after," I said then darted off.

My trip to the locker room gave me a chance to catch my breath before joining Alex on the elliptical machines.

"So I talked to the kids about you coming over on Friday."

"And what did they say?"

"Not much. But that's probably because I just told them you were an old friend from high school." I glanced at Alex, searching his face for some sort of reaction.

"That's okay. You'll tell them about us when you're ready," he said then raised an eyebrow at me. "There is still an us, right? You haven't changed your mind, have you?"

I shook my head. "No. I haven't. And I will tell Jakey and Lydia, but I think it's better if they meet you first before I spring the news about us on them."

I still had this weird sense of whiplash about Alex. Only twenty-four hours ago, he was just an old friend from high school, my workout buddy. And today he was, well, more. Although I supposed we had been more all along, and we'd just been too gun-shy to admit it to each other. Now that we had, every brush of his hand against mine felt turbocharged. When he reached out to correct my form on the weight machines, I had to hold in a gasp.

BY THE TIME Friday rolled around, I was a nervous ball of energy. The combo of sort-of-first-date jitters—even though technically that wasn't what dinner was going to be—mixed with my apprehension about introducing Alex to the kids had my anxiety in overdrive.

I started cooking dinner probably an hour before I should have just to keep my hands and mind busy. By the time Alex arrived at eight, the table was set and dinner—chicken piccata and salad—was ready.

"It smells really good in here," Alex said as I let him in.

"I hope you're hungry."

He smiled. "I'm starving actually."

Alex followed me inside. Jacob and Lydia got up from the couch and slowly walked over to me.

"This is the friend I was telling you guys about the other day," I said to them.

They both gave Alex a sheepish look. Lydia stood behind me, holding onto one of my hands. She was a sweet girl but super shy, just like I'd been at her age.

"You must be Lydia," Alex said, taking a step closer.

She nodded but said nothing.

"I brought you something." He turned his head in Jacob's direction. "You too."

"What is it?" Jacob asked eagerly.

"Dessert." Alex reached into the pocket of his jacket and produced two bags of sour gummies.

"Yay, gummies!" Lydia finally stopped hiding behind me to take a closer look at Alex's offering.

"Hand them over." I took the bags from Alex before the kids could reach them. "Dinner before candy. Wash your hands and then go sit down."

"Thank you," Jacob said to Alex, remembering his manners.

When they scurried off to the bathroom, I said, "Since when is candy dessert?"

"I couldn't help myself. You know I'm trying to win them over."

"Mission accomplished." For a man with no children, Alex seemed to know an awful lot about them.

After everyone finished washing their hands, we all sat down to eat. Alex looked across the table at Jacob and Lydia. "So, I hear you guys both play soccer."

"Yeah, but I'm not very good at it," Jacob said.

"Soccer wasn't my thing, either, when I was your age," Alex said. "But if you weren't playing soccer, then what else would you be doing?"

Jacob shrugged. "I don't really know. Maybe band if Mommy lets me."

"I was in band," Alex said. "All through high school."

"That's right," I said, remembering Alex lugging his instrument to and from school. "You played the saxophone, right?"

"Yup." He glanced at Lydia. "What about you? Do you like music too?"

She shook her head. "I like gymnastics."

"She just started going last year," I explained.

"Gymnastics? Wow. I bet you're really good at it."

Lydia just smiled, too shy to agree that he was right.

I sat there listening while the three of them chatted, enjoying Alex's effort to get to know my kids better. By the end of dinner, it was obvious that they both really liked him and not just because he'd brought them sour gummy worms. After we finished eating, I gave Jacob and Lydia each their bag of candy. They took them to the couch and turned on the TV while Alex helped me clean up.

"They're sweet kids," Alex said.

"They seem to really like you." I bent down to fill the dishwasher with dirty forks and knives. "Of course, that might just be because you bribed them with candy."

"You're not really mad at me for that, are you?"

I smiled and shook my head. "Of course not," I said. "But try not to make it a regular thing. Lydia's got a sweet tooth the size of California."

Alex laughed. "What kid doesn't?"

"I suppose you have a point."

"You're a good mom. I can tell. Those kids adore you."

"I'm all they have, and I adore them right back."

Once Alex and I were done clearing off the table, we joined the kids on the couch. They were watching one of their favorite *Nick Jr.* shows, but before it finished, Lydia fell asleep with her head on my lap. I carried her into her bedroom and took off her clothes, replacing them with pajamas. By the time I rejoined Alex and Jacob, they were deep in a discussion about which video games were their favorites.

"Jakey, it's time to get ready for bed," I said.

He frowned. "Why? There's no school tomorrow."

"Because it's after ten o'clock."

"How is it that late already?" Alex ran a hand through his hair. "I should probably get going."

"Go put on your pajamas," I told Jacob. "I'm going to walk Alex to the door, and then I'll come say good night."

"It was nice meeting you," Alex said, holding his hand out for Jacob to shake.

"Nice meeting you too."

"Next time we'll have to play a few rounds of *Super Smash Bros.*"

Jacob's eyes lit up. "Really? When?"

"Pajamas, Jakey. We can talk about when Alex is coming back another time."

He slumped off down the hallway. I turned to Alex and smiled. "First candy, now video games. You really know what you're doing."

He just shrugged.

"C'mon. I'll walk you outside."

He followed me to the door. Once we stepped outside, he turned to face me. "I had a really nice time tonight."

"So did I."

He leaned in to give me a kiss. It lasted only a moment, but it was enough to send my heart racing.

"Will I see you on Monday at the gym?" he asked.

"Yeah. I'll be there."

He shoved his hands into the pockets of his jeans. "I really wish I could take you out to dinner. Just me and you. Do you think I could sometime?"

"Yes, but I'm not sure when. The kids have school all week, so I've got to get them in bed by eight. So maybe next weekend. I'll ask my friend Marla if she can babysit."

"I understand. No pressure. You just let me know when you can."

Alex walked over to the driveway and got in his car. I stood in the doorway, smiling as I watched him drive away, pleased that the night had gone even better than I'd hoped it would.

It was too late to call Marla. But the next morning, right after the kids and I finished breakfast, I texted her

I've got news.

What is it???

Alex and I are dating.

My phone rang a moment later. As soon as I answered, Marla practically squealed in my ear. "I knew it, I knew it, I knew it."

"He came over last night to meet the kids."

"And?"

"It went well."

"So when are you guys going to go out on your first real date?"

"Whenever I can get a babysitter to watch the kids."

"Excuse me. What am I? Chopped liver?"

"Are you sure you wouldn't mind?"

"Of course not," she said. "Just let me know when."

"I feel kind of bad. What if the kids think Alex is more

important to me than they are?"

"You're with them every day," she said. "I only get my kids half the time, and they still know how much I love them. Plus, it's not like you're leaving them with a stranger. They'll be with Auntie Marla." When I didn't answer, Marla continued. "Everybody needs a break sometimes. Even you."

"Thanks, Marla. I really appreciate it."

As soon as I got off the phone with her, I called Alex.

"Marla agreed to babysit the kids. I just need to let her know when you want to go out."

"My schedule is wide open. We can go out right now if you want to."

I laughed. "I just barely finished breakfast."

"Dinner then?"

"How about next Saturday instead?" I suggested. "I can't very well ask Marla to drop everything for me. She's going to need a little advance notice."

"All right," he said. "I think I can manage to wait seven more days but only because I get to see you on Monday."

ONE WEEK LATER, I brought the kids over to Marla's at around five to give myself enough time to get ready for my date with Alex. Less than fifteen minutes later, the doorbell rang.

"I know I'm a little early," he said as I let him in.

I'd just finished combing my hair. "That's all right. I'm pretty much ready."

"You look ... stunning."

"Thank you." I managed a smile despite my nerves. It didn't matter that I'd known Alex for years, I couldn't shake that jittery feeling that filled my chest every time I was around him.

A few minutes later, we got into his car. He drove us to a small French café that I'd suggested for dinner.

The restaurant was casual, a perfect fit for us since, like me, Alex preferred comfort over style, although I had gotten a little dressed up. I wore dark denim jeans and a black short-sleeved blouse, and I'd put on eyeshadow and lip gloss. My hair was down, a change from the ponytail that was pretty much a necessity when I worked out.

The host showed us to a table, handed us menus, and walked away after promising a server would be with us shortly.

"Do you have any menu suggestions?" Alex asked.

"The lamb is amazing."

"Sounds good." Alex set his menu down on the table and lifted his gaze to meet mine. "Did you used to come here with your husband?"

I hesitated before replying. "We came here once together. It was a long time ago, though. Ryan wasn't much of a French food fan."

"I'm sorry. I shouldn't have asked you that. I don't know what I was thinking." He looked away.

"Hey," I said, waiting for Alex to meet my gaze again before continuing. "We both have pasts. It makes no sense pretending we don't."

"Yeah, I know. But things weren't great between you and your husband. I don't want to bring up bad memories. Not on our first date."

"It's okay," I said. "If you have questions, I don't mind answering them."

Just then our server walked up and introduced himself. He filled our glasses with water and took our orders. After he walked away, I said, "Where were we?"

"We were talking about Ryan."

"Right." Talking about previous relationships was supposed to be a no-no on a first date, but I could tell Alex had questions, and I didn't mind them. "So, what do you want to know?"

"What do you think went wrong between the two of you?"

I considered his question carefully. There was no easy answer. It seemed like most people assumed that as long as your husband had a job and didn't hit you or cheat on you, it meant you'd scored, at the very least, an acceptable husband. Ryan didn't do any of those things, but I felt far from lucky to have been married to him.

"Well, there were the usual things a lot of women complain about. He barely helped around the house, and he spent money like it was going out of style. We fought about that a lot in the beginning, especially after the kids were born, but I could've dealt with that stuff. Ryan's biggest problem was that he could be downright mean. And he had a wicked temper. When he got into one of his moods, no one wanted to be around him. Of course, he picked up on that, and it only made him angrier. When Ryan got mad, Jacob and I got the brunt of it." I paused and shook my head. They were not happy memories. "He'd say the ugliest, most-hurtful things."

Alex reached across the table for my hand.

"I'm sorry you went through that."

I managed a weak smile. "So am I."

A long silence descended. Perhaps Alex regretted the question, or maybe my answer had been more than he'd expected. The server came with our food, breaking the tension.

I took a bite of my steak, savoring the juicy, salty flavor.

"What about you?" I asked. "Why do you suppose your ex cheated? Did she ever tell you?"

He shrugged. "I was never enough for her. If I brought her flowers, she'd ask why they weren't roses. If I gave her jewelry, she'd want to know how many carats. When we went on vacation, we'd have to stay at five-star resorts," he explained. "I worked all the time, and she didn't work at all, which left her with a lot of time on her hands. Time she apparently spent finding other guys who could give her the things I couldn't."

"How many guys are we talking?"

"I have no idea. And the truth is, I don't really care. At least not anymore. Kristi was all wrong for me, and I knew that, but I married her anyway. I'm just glad I don't have to deal with her anymore."

It was my turn to tell Alex how sorry I was.

"You know, we could've avoided all this heartbreak if we'd just eloped before my parents dragged me off to Pollock Pines."

I laughed. "We were seventeen, so it wouldn't have been legal," I said. "And besides, I didn't even know you liked me. At least not like that."

"Because I was too scared to tell you," Alex replied. He stared at me from across the table. "Do you know how many times I've thought about you over the past eighteen years?"

I shook my head.

"More than I can count. Even though I didn't think I'd ever see you again," he said. "It blew my mind that day when we ran into each other at the gym."

"Yeah." I smiled. "It kind of blew mine too."

He reached across the table for my hand. His touch made my heart race. One date and I was already falling. I kept thinking about that on the ride back to my house. This was not good, but at the same time *so* good.

Way too quickly, Alex arrived at my house and pulled into the driveway.

I turned to face him. "I had a really nice time."

"We're doing this again, right?"

I nodded, and a moment later, Alex reached for me. His hand went to the nape of my neck. For a moment, he just rested it there, but then he pulled me into a kiss. My insides spun and churned as he parted my lips to kiss me deeper, harder.

I pulled away. "Do you want to come inside for a bit?" I asked, hoping he didn't think I was inviting him in for sex. I wasn't ready for that, but I wanted to know how it would feel to have his arms around me, to rest my head on his chest and hear his heart beating. The kids were at Marla's, playing *Minecraft* and coloring. I didn't know when a chance for us to be alone together would come again.

"I'd like that."

We got out of the car, and Alex followed me inside. I flicked on the light switch and closed the door behind the two of us. Suddenly, I felt awkward, like I wasn't sure what we were supposed to do next. "Um, why don't we sit down?"

"Sure, that sounds like a good idea."

I smiled, realizing Alex was just as nervous as I was. "C'mon." I took his hand and led him to the couch. I turned the TV on and channel surfed. "Anything in particular you want to watch?"

"As long as it's not the news."

I settled on some Travel Channel show where the host visits other countries just to try their most disgusting food and pretend to enjoy it. Alex put his arm over my shoulder, and I nestled into him. After a few minutes, I looked up at him, and then we were kissing again. I'd missed this. Having a connection with someone. I'd long ago given up the idea of ever feeling this way again. Over time, I'd lost the spark that I once had for my husband. I went through the motions to keep him happy, but whenever Ryan and I were physical, I was completely detached. It was like another person was making love to him.

This thing with Alex felt different. And not just because we hadn't been together for very long. The beginning of my relationship with Ryan had felt like a blazing inferno. I was consumed with him. So consumed that I couldn't see anything except for how perfect I thought he was. With Alex, things felt more like a warm fire on a cold winter evening. The flames licked at me, heating every inch of my body, but they didn't burn me to the ground. The passion was there, but at the same time, I felt safe and protected.

I wrapped my arms around Alex. He whispered in my ear, "I want you so bad."

I tensed. I wasn't ready for this to happen. I pulled away. "I'm sorry, but I ... I'm not—"

"It's okay," he said. "I didn't actually think we were going to. Not tonight. I just wanted to let you know that I think you're super sexy, and whenever you're ready, so am I."

A huge sense of relief filled me. I wanted him, too, but I wanted to be smart and do things differently than I had with Ryan. My former self probably would have slept with Alex. But it was just too soon. I didn't want to jump into bed with him right away. "Thank you for understanding."

"I never want to do anything to make you feel uncomfortable."

I pulled him closer, kissed him again, and breathed in his scent, a light mix of lavender, probably from his laundry soap, and a woodsy cologne. I could've sat there, wrapped in his arms, for hours, but it was getting late. I had to bring the kids back from Marla's before they fell asleep. They were getting too heavy for me to carry them all the way from her house to mine.

"I should go pick up the kids."

"Will you call me tomorrow?" Alex asked.

I lifted my head to look up at him. "I will."

He gave me another kiss. Then I walked him to the door. He turned and wrapped his arms around me again. "One last kiss," he whispered into my ear. His breath on my neck gave me goosebumps. I pressed my lips on his, wishing that our time together didn't have to end so soon.

15

All week, I went back and forth trying to decide whether or not to tell the kids that Alex and I were together. I worried that they'd think I was trying to replace their father. And I worried that it was too soon after Ryan's death, but I didn't want to lie to my kids either. I asked Marla what she thought, then Lynette, and finally Alex.

"Like I told you before, I'm okay with waiting until you're ready to tell them about us," he said. "Even if that means I don't get to see you as often."

"What if I said I don't want to wait?"

"That's fine too." Alex was trying to keep a serious face, but I swore I saw a smile in his eyes.

"I was thinking of taking the kids to Fairytale Town on Saturday and then Vic's for ice cream after. Maybe you can come with us?"

"I'd like that." We'd just finished working out and were standing in front of my car. Alex inched closer to me, resting his hands on my hips.

"We can tell them about us together."

"You sure that's how you want to do it?"

I shrugged. "The kids might have questions for both of us."

"You've got a point."

"So it's a date?"

Alex smiled. I wrapped my hands around the nape of his neck. He gave me a kiss. "It's a date."

FAIRYTALE TOWN WAS a park with slides and play structures inspired by fairytales like "Mother Goose" and "Jack and the Beanstalk." It was a good and inexpensive way to keep the kids busy for an afternoon. With the loss of Ryan's pay, I couldn't afford weekend trips to Lake Tahoe or the coast. Although even if I had the money, the winding roads up in the mountains or the hills in San Francisco were too frightening for me to navigate. Ryan had always been the one to drive because, the few times I had, he always found something to criticize.

The chilly morning had given way to a clear, sunny, and hot afternoon. Since the kids had met Alex once before, they seemed less shy this time. They ran around the park while Alex and I sat on a bench close enough for me to keep an eye on them. As I watched them play, I couldn't help but think about the way time had flown by so darn quick. It was cliché, but it really did feel like only yesterday since I'd held my babies in my arms. And now, Jacob was only a few years from being a teenager.

For the past few years, I'd imagined that when the kids were grown, I'd find the courage to tell Ryan I wanted a divorce. I'd be lonely after they left home, but as sad as the thought made me, it was better than the prospect of enduring Ryan for the rest of my life. I'd resigned myself to that future. But now, I was slowly beginning to imagine a different and better future for myself.

By one o'clock, Jacob and Lydia were hungry and thirsty and worn out from the heat.

"Who's ready to go to Vic's?" I asked.

"Me," the kids said in unison.

As they gulped down virgin lime rickeys and grilled cheese sandwiches, I geared up to tell them why Alex was with us. But before I did that, we needed ice cream. It was, after all, what Vic's was famous for.

"So, there's something I wanted to tell you guys about me and Alex," I said.

"What is it?" Jacob asked.

I glanced at Alex out of the corner of my eye. He gave me a slight nod, encouraging me to go on. "Alex and I are dating."

"I knew it," Jacob said, sounding more satisfied with himself than anything. He looked at his sister. "Didn't I tell you?"

"How do you feel about it?"

"Good," Lydia said, smiling. "I like Alex."

"Thank you," he replied, giving her a thumbs-up.

"I like you too," Jacob said.

"So that means you're okay that Alex came with us today?"

Jacob and Lydia both nodded.

"Do you have any questions you want to ask me?" Alex asked. "I'd love for the two of you to get to know me better and vice versa."

"What should we call you?" Jacob asked.

"Alex is perfectly fine."

"Do you love my mommy?" Lydia asked.

My face heated. I hadn't expected her to ask such a blunt question, but it really shouldn't have surprised me. Like most kids, Lydia just said whatever came to her mind.

"I care about your mommy very much."

That answer seemed to satisfy Lydia. The kids didn't have much more to say after that. They were too busy enjoying their ice cream. But when we got home later, I was met with a barrage of questions.

"Do we have to do whatever Alex tells us to?"

"How much time are you going to spend with him?"

"Are you guys going to get married?"

"Are you going to have another baby?"

I did my best to answer. "I want you to know that even though Mommy has a boyfriend, you two come first, no matter what."

"We know, Mommy," Jacob said.

I gave them both a hug.

When I went to bed that night, I lay there thinking things over. I was still filled with regret and guilt over Ryan, but time had helped to ease some of those feelings, and the kids and Alex distracted me from my most miserable thoughts. It had been a very long time since my life had hummed along as smoothly as it had over the past few weeks. I just prayed that the ride would last.

16

Alex and I began cheating on our workouts, cutting them short so we could kiss and touch in my car or his before we headed off to work. It was the only chance we had to be intimate. Around the kids, we never did more than hold hands. Thanks to Marla, we even managed to meet for dinner again.

Alex invited me to his house after. I agreed even though I wasn't ready to get into bed with him just yet. Thankfully he sensed that and didn't push. It had been over ten years since I'd had sex with anyone other than Ryan. The prospect made me nervous, but one morning, I realized I was ready. I'd gotten to the point where I couldn't stop thinking about how it would feel to have Alex make love to me. I longed for that feeling, the heat, the rush of emotions.

On a Saturday morning, Marla called to invite Jacob and Lydia to a movie with her kids. I insisted on coming along, but she was even more insistent that I use the free time to my advantage and spend it with Alex.

While the kids were getting ready, I texted him.

Are you busy today?

Why? Do you have something in mind?

Marla's taking the kids to the movies in a few minutes. I thought you might like to come over.

I'm already running out to my car.

He arrived a few minutes after Marla left with Jacob and Lydia. I was waiting by the door and flung it open the second he knocked. We had at least two and half hours, maybe even three, before the kids returned home. I planned on taking advantage because who knew when we'd get a block of time together like that again? I grabbed Alex's hand and pulled him over to the couch. As soon as he sat down, I kissed him.

"God, I've missed you," he said, running his hands through my hair.

"You just saw me yesterday."

"That's different. I can't do this when there are people around." He drew me closer and pressed his lips on mine again. Then he pulled me onto his lap. His arm went around my back. As it did, his phone fell out of his back pocket. He picked it up and laid it on the coffee table before turning his attention back to me. He kissed my neck, tracing his lips along the sensitive skin and bringing out goosebumps all over my flesh. I reached under his shirt, pressing my palms flat against his back. His breath hitched. We both knew where this was headed. It would be a long time before we'd get this much kid-free time with each other again.

Alex broke our kiss. He clasped my face in his hands, his fingers threaded through my hair, and looked into my eyes. "Have I told you how much you mean to me?"

"You may have mentioned it a time or two."

"It's true. I really mean it. Sometimes I think I should have told you all those years ago, but maybe it was meant to be this way. Maybe we were meant to learn a thing or two about relationships before finding each other."

"I don't know. I could've really skipped over the whole fall-ing-for-the-wrong-guy chapter of my life."

"Believe me, I know how you feel. I could've done without that part too." Alex just stared into my eyes for another moment. I could tell he had something on the tip of his tongue. He finally said, "I thought about you a lot over the years. I wondered what my life would've been like if I'd married you instead."

I couldn't exactly say the same thing. I'd liked Alex in high school, but he was too out of my reach, or at least that's what I'd thought back then, so I hadn't bothered to actually entertain any fantasy about there ever being anything between us. Yet now here we were, almost twenty years later, and he was sitting on my couch, and I was sitting on his lap. His hands were still in my hair, and mine were wrapped around his shoulders. I leaned in for another kiss. Flames licked my insides as his tongue parted my lips. Alex leaned into me, pressing me down until my back rested on the couch. We kissed for a few more minutes. Then he pulled away.

"Do you mind if I use your bathroom?"

"Of course not. You know where it is, right?"

He nodded. Alex got up from the couch and headed down the hallway. I sat up, smiling, eager for him to come back.

His phone, which he'd left on the coffee table, rang. "Alex," I called out. "You've got a call."

"Can you answer it? Just tell whoever it is to hold on."

Even though it was what Alex wanted me to do, I hesitated before picking up his phone. "Hello," I said.

"Um, is my dad there?"

"Your dad?"

I was about to tell whoever it was that they'd got the wrong number when the girl on the other end of the line said, "Yeah, my dad, Alex."

I couldn't find any words.

"Hello," the girl said.

I managed to choke out. "Just a minute."

Alex had just returned from the bathroom. In a daze, I stood up and handed him the phone.

"Who is it?" he mouthed.

"It's … it's your daughter." *The one you told me you didn't have.*

I couldn't decipher his expression. He took the phone and pressed it to his ear, then he turned his back to me. Not that it mattered. I had no intention of standing there and listening in on his conversation. Instead, I headed down the hallway and into my bedroom, closing the door behind myself.

I sat on my bed, hoping Alex was smart enough to just leave without trying to explain why he'd lied to me. But after a few minutes, he knocked on my door.

"Go away," I said, fuming.

He opened the door, and I cursed myself for not locking it. "It's not what you think," he said, walking over to me.

"What I think is that you're a liar." I stared up at him, picturing his daughter with Alex's beautiful blue eyes, and tried to imagine why he would deny her. What kind of person would do something like that? "You told me more than once that you didn't have any children."

"No, I didn't," Alex insisted.

He hadn't come right out and said those specific words, but he had to know that's what I assumed giving everything else he'd said. "You told me that you didn't think you could have a child. Clearly that was a lie."

"I didn't lie. Leah isn't my daughter. At least not technically."

"So, her name is Leah?"

He nodded. "Yes."

"Is she your stepdaughter?"

He shook his head.

"If she's not your daughter, then why did she refer to you as her dad?"

"Because that's what she thinks I am."

"What are you not telling me?" I asked, my building frustration causing my voice to rise.

He stared at me for a moment before answering. "Kristi cheated on me. Leah isn't my daughter, at least not biologically. I only found out a few months ago while we were in the middle of our divorce."

My first instinct was to reach for his hand and comfort him. But as bad as I felt for him, that didn't excuse his lie. "Biology aside, she's still your daughter," I said. "We've been dating for a few weeks, not to mention all the time we spent together before that, and you haven't said a word about her."

He ran a hand through his hair. "This situation is so hard for me to talk about."

I shook my head and took a few steps backward. "I don't think I can do this, Alex. Relationships require trust. You didn't trust me enough to tell me about Leah, and now that I found out about her, I feel like I can't trust you."

"I was going to tell you eventually."

I wanted to believe him, but how could I? Tears formed in the corners of my eyes. I fought them back. I did not want Alex to see me cry.

This was ridiculous, we'd only been dating a few weeks. Why was I so broken up over some lie? I reminded myself that when I'd agreed to give us a chance, I'd asked him not to lie to me, and he'd promised he wouldn't. But he had anyway. I couldn't trust him. If he could lie about something major like whether or not he had children, then he could lie about anything. I did not need that in my life.

Alex just stood there pleading with his eyes.

"I want you to leave."

"Vanessa, please don't do this. I'm sorry, I really am. I know I should've told you sooner, but—"

"There's nothing left to say." I crossed my arms. "I can't be with someone I don't trust."

"Vanessa—"

"I asked you to leave."

He must've heard the anger in my voice because, after staring at me for a moment, he finally said, "I'll go. But it's not over. It can't be. You have to give me another chance."

Alex turned and walked away. After I heard the front door shut behind him, I let out the breath I hadn't even realized I was holding. I wiped my eyes with the back of my trembling hands. I didn't want the kids to see that I was upset when they returned home later.

While I waited for Marla to come back, I thought about how I was going to explain to the kids that Alex wasn't Mommy's boyfriend anymore. The thought made me sick to my stomach. Jacob and Lydia really liked him. They'd already been through so much emotional turmoil in their lives. Those years of hearing their mom and dad argue were bad enough, then they'd had to grieve the death of their father, and now, just as they'd welcomed someone new into their lives, I was going to have to turn things upside down for them, again. I wished I'd never introduced them to Alex. I wished I hadn't let him talk me into giving him a chance. I was right when I'd told Marla I didn't know what I was doing when it came to men. Somehow, I always chose wrong. I'd only given Alex a chance because things were supposed to be different with him.

I busied myself with cleaning the house to keep my mind off Alex. Two hours later, Marla returned. Her kids and mine ran into the house, buzzing with excitement thanks to the sugar from all the soda and candy they'd had at the theater.

"Thank you for taking them to the movies," I said to Marla

after she followed them inside.

"No need to thank me. We had a good time. Right, guys?"

"Yeah," all five of them shouted together.

"How was the movie?" I asked.

"It was really good," Jacob said.

I turned to Lydia. "Did you like it too?"

"Yeah."

I smiled. It was rare that they both enjoyed the same things these days. I glanced at the clock. It was close to five. "Do you guys want me to make spaghetti for dinner? Or are you still too full of candy and popcorn?"

"I'm never too full for spaghetti," Jacob said.

"Me neither," his sister agreed. "I can help you make it if you want me to."

She was always asking to do things with me in the kitchen. But six was a little too young to be chopping onions or filling heavy pots full of water. "It's okay. I got it under control. Why don't you and Jacob go play with Abby and her brothers? I'll call you when dinner is ready."

The kids took off down the hallway. I started pulling out all the ingredients I needed for dinner. "You're staying for dinner, right?" I asked, looking over my shoulder at Marla.

"Sure." She took a seat at the table. "So how'd things go with Alex?"

"Not good. It's over between us."

Marla's eyes widened. "What? How come?"

"He's a liar. And I'm not interested in dating someone I can't trust."

"Good grief." She ran a hand through her hair. "You were supposed to be telling me about the mind-blowing sex you and Alex had for the first time. Not that you guys broke up. What exactly did he lie about?"

"He told me more than once that he doesn't have any children. But he actually does." I bit my lip. Just thinking about it made me boil over with anger. "A daughter named Leah."

Marla's jaw dropped. "How did you find out?"

I told her about Alex asking me to answer his phone while he was in the bathroom.

"I bet he wishes he never told you to do that."

"I'm glad he did because, if he hadn't, I wouldn't have found out the truth."

"Did he tell you why he lied? He's got to have a reason."

"His ex-wife cheated on him, so Leah is not biologically his. Apparently he only found out a few months ago, which is why he didn't tell me. He said it was too hard for him to talk about."

"That makes sense."

"I don't trust him anymore." The thought made me sad. I shook my head. "The truth is, I should've never agreed to go out with him in the first place. I knew something like this would happen. It's like I told you, I'm no good at choosing men. I had no business even trying."

"I've dated half a dozen men since my divorce," she said, "and they've all been jerks. Alex is different. You shouldn't throw away what the two of you have without giving him another chance."

"You're supposed to be on my side. Not Alex's."

"I'm not taking his side. I'm just telling you not to be so quick to pass judgment."

The sound of footsteps coming down the hallway stopped our conversation short. Jacob led the way into the living room with Lydia and Marla's kids trailing behind him. He turned on the TV.

"Is it okay if we play *Super Smash Bros* for a while?"

"Sure," I said, thankful for the interruption. Talking about Alex was only making me feel worse. I was so angry and hurt that I didn't even want to think about him.

17

Alex waited until Monday to call. Maybe he thought giving me some time would help me to calm down. But time hadn't changed anything. The sound of his voice on the other end of the phone made me boil over again.

"Why are you calling? I told you it was over."

"We need to talk. You have to give me a chance to explain."

"I already did."

"There's a lot more to this story."

"Then go ahead. I'm listening."

"Not over the phone. It has to be in person."

"No, that's not happening." I hung up before he could respond. One look into those blue eyes of his and I'd be done. He'd come up with some excuse for his lies, and I'd forgive him because, no matter how angry I was, I had feelings for him that I couldn't just turn off no matter how badly I wanted to. That's what had happened with Ryan. He'd thrown so many red flags at me while we'd dated, but every time I got close to walking away, he'd plead with me to stay. I could not make a mistake like that again, especially now that there was more than my heart at stake. I had to think about Jacob and Lydia. And there was also Alex's daughter Leah to consider.

For the next few hours, my anger and pain fueled me, helping me get through hours of sifting through emails and returning calls. But when the time came for me to pick up the kids from school, I was mentally and physically drained, even though the day was barely half over. I made the kids frozen pizza and chicken nuggets for dinner rather than cooking them a real meal. By the end of the week, I finally realized something. I wasn't angry anymore. My heart just plain hurt. I struggled to keep from crying. There was an emptiness inside of me, and nothing I did helped to fill it.

To make things worse, that awful voice inside my head returned, telling me I deserved the heartache. I'd promised Ryan that if he passed before me, I wouldn't be with anyone else. Although, back then, I never really imagined that Ryan would die at such a young age.

But despite that voice, I found myself thinking about Alex more often than I wanted. I missed our morning workouts and the conversations that came with them. But more than anything, I missed the way his lips felt on mine. Every time I realized where my mind had taken me, I shook my head, willing all thoughts of Alex out of my mind. I didn't need them, and I didn't need him.

It would have been infinitely easier to put Alex behind me if it weren't for his daily calls. Every time the screen of my phone lit up with his number, I had to fight with myself not to answer. It didn't help that Marla kept bugging me about giving him a chance.

"I can't be in a relationship without trust," I told her for the hundredth time.

"I swear you're the most stubborn person I know," she said.

A week passed before I woke up one morning and realized

that I wasn't going to be able to put Alex behind me without hearing the part of story he hadn't had a chance to tell me before I'd kicked him out of my house. Marla had gotten to me and time had given me some perspective. Maybe I was being too hard on Alex. I missed him more than I wanted to. No matter how hard I'd tried, I couldn't get him out of my head. I got out of bed and texted Marla.

Any chance you can watch Jacob and Lydia for a bit?

If this means that you're finally listening to me about talking to Alex, then Yes!!!

Yes, that's what it means.

Ok. I'll be over in a bit. I made plans with Lynette, so she's coming too if that's ok with you.

Of course it is.

I texted Alex next.

Will you be home today? I can come by if you still want to talk.

Yes, I'll be home, and yes, I still want to talk. Do you remember where I live?

Yes.

I got dressed and went into the kitchen to make breakfast. Just as I finished loading the dishwasher, Marla and Lynette arrived. Marla's kids were with her ex, but Lynette had brought her daughter. I hadn't told Jacob and Lydia they were coming over, and the two of them were excited by the surprise visit.

"My mommy's got a date," I heard Lydia whisper to Isabel.

I still hadn't told them that Alex and I had broken up. Every time I'd tried, I couldn't come up with the right words.

It was May, which in Sacramento meant summer temperatures, so I slipped my feet into a pair of flip-flops.

"Get going, girl." Marla grabbed my purse, which hung from the doorknob of the coat closet, and handed it to me. "And take as much time as you need."

"Yes," Lynette chimed in. "Because I won't be able to pry Isabel away from Lydia for at least a few hours."

I loved Marla and Lynette like they were my sisters. "You guys are the best."

"Jacob, Lydia," I called out. They lifted their heads to see what I wanted. "I won't be gone long. You two listen to Marla and Lynette, okay?"

ALEX'S HOUSE was only a few minutes' drive from mine. He lived in the Garden of the Gods section of Sacramento, a neighborhood with homes built in the 1950s and streets with names like Adonis Way, Venus Drive, and Daphne Avenue. It was a typical middle-class neighborhood, like mine, but Alex's home had been remodeled before he'd moved into it, and it had a lot of high-end features that mine didn't. I parked my car in his driveway and walked up to the front door with my heart pounding in my chest. For a moment, I contemplated turning around and going back home. Instead, I lifted my hand and rang the doorbell. A moment later, Alex answered.

"You came," he said, running a hand through his messy hair.

I refused to let the somber expression on his face sway me. "You said you wanted to talk, so here I am." I stepped inside. It was a sunny day, but the shades in his house were down, so it was dark inside. He hadn't shaved. A five o'clock shadow actually looked good on him. It wasn't fair that he looked as handsome as ever with almost no effort. Not that it mattered. I wasn't going to let that sway me.

"You want to sit down?" he asked.

"Sure." I followed him into the living room and took a seat on the couch. I folded my arms over my chest. He sat beside me.

For a moment, neither of us said anything. Then Alex said,

"I'm sorry I lied." He looked away. "Like I said, this is hard to talk about."

I waited for him to continue. When he didn't, I said, "Go on."

"While Kristi and I were going through our divorce, I asked for joint custody, but Kristi wouldn't agree. I told her I'd fight for it. That's when she told me the truth. Leah isn't mine. Her real dad was some guy she cheated on me with years ago."

His pained expression tore at my heart. "I'm sorry, Alex."

"It was devastating, but I told Kristi it didn't matter, that I still wanted joint custody. So she said if I fought her for it, she'd tell Leah I wasn't her father. I didn't want to do that to my little girl. She's only eleven, and she's already been through so much, her parents fighting all the time then splitting up. Kristi promised that if I agreed to let her have primary custody of Leah, she wouldn't tell her the truth until we both agreed on the right time and way to do it. She also promised I'd get to see Leah whenever I wanted. But it hasn't exactly turned out that way."

"What do you mean?"

"Kristi's always got some sort of reason why I can't see Leah. And she's filling our daughter's head with all kinds of lies. She's got Leah convinced she has no idea why I left. Last time I talked to Kristi, she basically said that if I really wanted time with Leah, then I'd forgive her for cheating. She wants things to go back to the way they were before I found out."

"How can she expect that after everything she's put you through?"

"Kristi lives in her own personal fantasy world where she can say and do whatever she wants and whoever she hurts will just magically get over it."

I could relate to that. Ryan had never cheated on me, but he believed he could do no wrong, that just by virtue of being married I should forgive him when he treated me badly.

"What if your ex is lying to you about Leah?" I asked.

Alex shook his head. "She's not. Believe me, if I had so much as the smallest doubt, I would've demanded a DNA test. But I'm not going to put Leah through that for nothing."

"How can you be so sure?"

"Leah looks nothing like me. I've always kind of suspected, but I never wanted to admit it to myself. I loved that girl from the second she came into this world, and I always will."

"You can't let Kristi get away with what she's doing, though. It's not right."

"Kristi doesn't make idle threats. If I push too hard, she'll tell her version of the truth to Leah and break our daughter's heart just to spite me."

"And if you don't, Leah will grow up thinking you're some deadbeat dad who ran out on her and her mother and doesn't care to make the time to see his child. That can't be what you want. Biology or not, you're Leah's father in every way that counts."

"Of course it's not what I want."

"I'm telling you from personal experience that having a parent abandon you hurts. A lot."

He shook his head then lowered it into his open palms. My heart hurt for him. "I wish I knew what the right thing to do was. I thought I was protecting Leah, but oh my God, you should have heard her voice on the phone last week. She's so sad. And on top of that, I screwed things up between us and ran you off. I swear I'm such a fuck up."

I put my hand on his back. "No, you're not."

"When you mentioned me having a house full of kids one day I was still so bitter about everything that went down between Kristi and I that I couldn't bring myself to tell you about Leah. I realized I mislead you, but I planned on telling you about her at some point, I swear I did." He shook his head. "I could never think of the right words to say, though. And then all this time passed, and I knew you'd be mad at me for not being honest, so I kept chickening out of telling you the truth. I'm sorry I lied, and I'm sorry I ruined things between us."

"You didn't ruin things."

He lifted his head and looked at me. "I didn't?"

I told myself I wasn't being an idiot. His story made sense. I understood why he'd deceived me. This was something we could put behind us. It had to be, because now that my anger had dissipated, I missed him terribly. "I should've given you a chance to explain all this before breaking up with you."

"And I should've told you the truth sooner."

"Yeah, you should've, but I guess I understand why you didn't."

"So that means you forgive me?" Alex asked, his expression hopeful.

I nodded.

He shook his head. "I thought I lost you, Vanessa. I've been going crazy all week."

I moved closer to him, putting my hand on the nape of his neck. The look in his eyes tore at me. I was scared to death of forgiving him, but I couldn't bring myself to walk away. "I've been going crazy too. I felt ... empty without you."

As soon as those words were out, his lips were on mine. It felt like a bolt of lightning ran through me. Alex deepened the kiss, pulling me closer. I ran my hands through his hair. I wanted to touch every inch of his body, and I wanted him to do the same to mine. In the space of a few minutes, I'd felt closer to him than I ever had. I was overcome with emotions. My problems with Ryan were different than the ones Alex had with his ex-wife, but I knew how it felt to be hurt by the person you once loved, the person you'd given your heart to. Just like Alex did. I wanted to make things better for him, and I wanted him to do the same for me. Together we could heal each other.

"Oh God, Vanessa, you have no idea what you're doing to me," he whispered in my ear.

I just kept kissing him, my lips traveling the length of his neck. I reached for the hem of his shirt and lifted it. He finished the job, yanking it over his head in one swift motion. I ran my hands over his sculpted chest and felt his heart drumming under my fingertips.

"Are you sure you want to do this?"

"Yes." I kissed him again.

He lifted me in his arms in one swift motion and carried me down the hall and into his bedroom. He slammed the door shut behind us before laying me down on his bed and making me feel things I hadn't in a very long time.

After, as I lay in Alex's arms, he apologized again.

"I'm really sorry that I lied to you, Vanessa. I promise it won't happen again."

"I believe you."

Alex eased me off his chest and turned on his side, propping his head up with his arm so he could look down at me. "You know what else I'm sorry for?" I shook my head, and he continued. "That someone hurt you so much that you don't trust yourself anymore."

I wondered how he knew. It was like he had reached inside my head and read my thoughts. "My bullshit radar sucks."

"Which was part of the reason why you were so angry with me?" he asked tucking a few stray hairs behind my ear.

I nodded.

"I could promise you that I'm different, but that would just be words," he said. "Instead, I'm going to show you. Every single day for as long as you let me. And if I somehow screw up and say or do something stupid, then I promise I'll fix it. You just have to give me the chance."

I smiled. "I will. Or at least I'll try to. I'll remind myself that you're the same Alex you were back in high school. It's been a long time, but you haven't changed." I might've doubted that at first, but after what he'd just told me about Leah and the way he struggled to do the right thing by her no matter how much it hurt him, I realized it was true. He was a good man. One of a kind.

"I'd like to think I'm a little better looking than I was back then," Alex teased.

I ran my hands over his muscled chest and shoulders. "Why? Because of all this?"

He smiled. "You noticed?"

"Well, I'm not blind," I said. "But just so you know, I'd like you even if you didn't look like an underwear model."

"You think I look like an underwear model?"

Before I could answer, he pressed his lips on mine. He lowered himself on top of me. I felt him stiffen and realized that he wanted me again. The thought excited me. I wrapped my arms around him and pulled him closer, ready for him, but this time Alex took his time, touching me and teasing me with his lips and his tongue before making love to me again.

"Have I ever told you how beautiful you are?" he asked after, looking down at me in such an intimate way it made my face heat and my heart quicken.

"You've mentioned it a time or two." I didn't really see myself that way and hadn't since Jacob was born. Before I became a mother, guys had regularly stared at or hit on me, but having a baby strapped to your chest in a carrier changed things. Not that I cared. Being a mother was more important to me than attracting attention. And my troubles with Ryan had me so turned off by men in general that I didn't think I'd ever care again whether or not one of them found me attractive.

Alex kissed me before easing himself down beside me. I reached for his hand, lacing my fingers through his. My mind wandered as I lay there. Eventually my thoughts settled on Alex and his issues with his ex-wife and daughter. Biology or not, Leah was his. He'd raised her, and he obviously loved her. It wasn't fair that he didn't get to be a part of her life.

"What are you thinking about?" Alex asked.

"Your daughter." I looked up at him. "I think you should fight for her. You should ask for joint custody."

"You don't know how bad I want to. But I don't want Leah's world turned upside down."

"The truth won't be easy for her to hear at any age. You can't keep it from her forever." I laced my fingers through his. "Besides, it isn't fair for your ex to keep you away from your daughter. It's obvious Leah wants you in her life. She wouldn't be calling you if she didn't."

"I'm worried it's too late. The divorce papers and custody arrangement have already been signed. I can't undo that."

"No. But what you can do is get yourself a lawyer. One that will explain to the courts why you agreed to let Kristi have primary custody of Leah in the first place and help you fight to get your rights back."

Alex shook his head. "The thought of dragging Leah into a messy fight between her mother and me makes me sick. And when she finds out the truth—"

"It'll hurt. But barely getting to see you has to hurt too," I said. "It's not too late to do something about it. The sooner you find a lawyer, the better."

Alex stared into my eyes. "If I do, will you help me? Will you be by my side? Cause I'm not sure I could go through that alone."

"Don't worry." I pulled him into a kiss. "You won't have to."

18

Alex wanted to take me somewhere for lunch, but I'd already been gone far longer than I'd planned on, so somehow I managed to peel myself away from him.

"I wish you could stay longer," he said as he walked me to the door.

I turned and rested my hand on his chest. "I'll see you Monday, at the gym."

He gave me a kiss. Then I turned back around, got into my car, and drove home.

When I arrived, Marla not-so-subtly suggested to the kids that it was such a nice day that they really should go outside and play in the backyard for a bit. As soon as the patio door closed behind them, she spun around.

"So ... you've been gone for a while."

"Spill the beans," Lynette commanded.

I couldn't stop my smile.

"I take it that means you two made up," Marla said.

I bit my lower lip, remembering the way Alex's hands had felt on my body. "Yeah."

Marla put her hands on her hips. "So, what did Alex say?"

"I'm not sure I should tell. It's kind of personal."

"C'mon, it's not like we're going to tell him that you told us," Lynette urged.

"Okay. Fine." I took a seat on the couch. Marla and Lynette flanked either side of me. "Alex didn't find out that his ex-wife cheated on him and that Leah wasn't his biological daughter until they were going through their divorce. He wanted joint custody anyway, but his ex threatened to tell Leah the truth. She said if he agreed to give her primary custody, she'd keep her mouth shut and let him see Leah whenever he wanted. But she's apparently reneged on the second part of that promise."

Lynette put her hand to her mouth. "Oh my God."

"That explains why he didn't want to talk about Leah," Marla said.

"I probably shouldn't say more than that. This whole thing has been really hard on Alex."

"But you two are back on track, right?" Marla asked. "You can at least tell me that, can't you?"

"Yes, we are."

"Thanks to who?" Marla asked, a satisfied smile on her face.

I smiled back. "To you."

"Well, I'm just glad you're happy," Lynette said. "Because if anyone deserves to be, it's you."

I gave her a hug. "Thanks for helping watch the kids."

"It's no big deal. You know Isabel loves coming over here to play."

Marla, Lynette, and Isabel hung out for another hour. After they left, I sat back down on the couch in the living room and stared outside at the kids playing in the back yard. Lydia and Jacob were filthy from digging in the dirt. I was glad I hadn't told them that Alex and I had split up. I guessed a part of me had hoped that it wasn't for good.

It was such a beautiful day that I decided to fill two glasses with lemonade and bring them outside for the kids. While they played, I sat reading a book, but I was too distracted thinking about Alex to get through more than a few pages.

ALEX and I fell back into our usual routine. On Monday, after dropping the kids off at school, I drove to the gym, anxious to get back to exercising after skipping my workouts for a whole week. I didn't ask Alex any more questions about Leah, and he didn't mention her either. I figured when he was ready to talk about her, he would. It turned out I didn't have to wait long.

A few days later, halfway through our workout, he announced, "I hired a lawyer." His tone was so casual, like he was telling me he'd just bought a new grill for his backyard, but his eyes gave him away.

"You did? That's great. What did he say?"

"She, actually, her name's Linda Allen. She thinks I've got a good case."

"Oh, Alex." I pressed the pause button on the treadmill and slowed my pace. "That's amazing."

"I've got a huge battle ahead. But I'm ready to fight."

"So what's the first step?"

"Linda's filing a petition for joint custody with the courts in a few days. She's getting the paperwork ready as we speak."

I smiled. "I can't wait to meet your daughter."

Alex slowed his pace, eventually stopping and hopping off the treadmill. "I can't wait for you to meet her either. But it might not be for a while. When Kristi finds out what I'm doing, she's gonna be pissed. I'm kind of nervous about what she'll do."

"She can't *do* anything."

"She can tell Leah the truth. And then she'll tell Leah what a horrible person I am. Over and over. Leah lives with Kristi. She spends a lot of time around her. What if she starts believing her mom and doesn't want to see me?"

I jumped off my treadmill and took Alex's hand. "That's not going to happen. If anything, Leah will be pissed at her mother for talking bad about you."

"Oh God. I hope you're right."

"I am right," I said. "And when this is all over and you finally get to spend time with Leah again, we'll all go out to celebrate. You, me, and our kids."

"That sounds amazing. You have no idea how bad I want that to happen."

"It will."

He inched closer to me and leaned in, resting his forehead on mine. "Any chance we can cut this workout short and head back to my place?"

My face heated. I bit my lower lip. "I'll go get my things."

A few minutes later, I was in my car, racing over to Alex's house. He'd beat me there and was already unlocking his door by the time I pulled into his driveway. After he closed the door behind us, he pulled me closer and kissed me. I peeled his shirt off first then mine. Bit by bit, our clothes came off, falling to the floor and leaving a trail on the way to his bedroom. My heart thudded in my chest as he lay me down on his bed.

"You're so beautiful," he said, looking straight into my eyes.

What I saw in his expression sent my heart racing even more than it had been. I reached for him and wrapped my legs around his back. I wasn't as good with words as he was, but I knew how to show him what I was feeling.

"What if I call in sick to work today?" he asked later as we lay in each other's arms.

"I wish, but I've got a mountain of work to do today." I turned to my side to check my phone, which rested on Alex's bedside table. Time had gone by way faster than I'd wanted it to. "As a matter of fact, I should get going."

It was next to impossible to get my head back into work after my morning with Alex, but I didn't have much of a choice. The company I worked for had gone on a hiring spree, and I had a lot to catch up on. As soon as I picked up the kids from school, I went right back to my computer. It was next to the last week of school, and I needed to get as much work done as I could before summer break.

THE NEXT TWO weeks seemed to fly by. On the kids' last day of school, we celebrated with frozen yogurt. Alex had taken a half day off work to come with us. As I watched the kids pile gummy worms, sprinkles, and whipped cream on their frozen yogurt, he whispered to me, "I can't wait for Leah to meet Jacob and Lydia. I just know she'll love them. She's always complained about being an only child."

"If she's anything like you, they'll love her too."

"Love who, Mommy?" Lydia asked.

I hadn't realized she'd been close enough to hear. I glanced at Alex, wondering if it was okay to talk about Leah. He gave me a quick nod.

"I haven't told you guys this before, but Alex has a daughter. She's eleven, and her name is Leah."

Jacob furrowed his brow and looked up at Alex. "Wait, I thought you didn't have any kids."

"It's ... sort of complicated," Alex said.

Thankfully Jacob didn't press the issue.

"What's she like?" Lydia asked.

"She's a little bit shy, just like you. But she's really smart and kind."

"Is she already out of school for the summer?" Jacob asked. I could see the wheels turning in his head. He was probably already mentally planning a playdate with her. He loved having someone new to play video games with. He got tired of playing with his sister all the time since she was only six and beating her wasn't much of a challenge.

"I think she's got another week, actually," Alex replied. There were a handful of different school districts in the Sacramento area, and they all followed their own schedules.

"So if you and my mommy get married, then she'll be my stepsister, right?" Lydia asked.

I almost choked on the water I was drinking.

"Um, yeah. That's right," Alex said.

"Cool. I always wanted a sister." Lydia scooped a spoonful of frozen yogurt into her mouth.

I glanced at Alex out of the corner of my eye, wondering what he was thinking. We hadn't been dating long enough to even think about marriage, and he was on the cusp of an epic custody battle. For a moment, I pictured what it would be like. Me, Alex, and our kids spending lazy weekends in Monterey or having fun on the boardwalk in Santa Cruz, during the summer when it was over a hundred degrees in Sacramento. We'd watch as the kids splashed in the water at the shoreline, shrieking as the cold water lapped up their legs. It was a happy thought.

I wanted to press freeze and keep that mental image pinned in my mind like the kids' drawings I stuck on the refrigerator door with magnets. But what if things didn't wind up working out? I'd often thought that happiness was meant for other people. While I was married to Ryan, I'd come to accept that. Now that things were different, I couldn't help but worry that the strange streak of good luck I'd been having for the past few months would one day vanish.

19

On the last Monday in June, the kids started a week of camp at the Sacramento Zoo, and I received a phone call from the last person I expected to hear from. I didn't usually pick up the phone when I didn't recognize the number on caller ID, but with the kids in camp, I worried it was a counselor calling to tell me one of them had gotten injured.

"Is Vanessa there?" the man on the other end asked.

"Who's calling?"

"It's Rick, Ryan's brother," he replied. "I tried calling him, but his phone is disconnected. Can you give me his new number?"

"Rick?" I said. "How did you get this number?"

"Ryan gave it to me a while back."

"I ... I tried to get ahold of you a few months ago. Your dad too."

"Ryan didn't tell you?"

"Tell me what?"

"Dad had a stroke about a year ago."

"Oh," I said, "I had no idea. Is he okay?"

"He can't walk or talk anymore, so the hospital set him up in a nursing home."

I couldn't believe Ryan hadn't mentioned anything about it. But that explained why I hadn't been able to reach his father.

"What about you?" I asked. "Where have you been?"

"I just got back from overseas. I've been in Thailand for the past eight months."

"Thailand?" I couldn't help but wonder what he was doing over there, but I didn't ask. With Rick, it was better not to. The longer I stayed on the phone with him, the more likely he was to ask for something.

"It's a long story," he said. "Anyway, why were you trying to get ahold of me? Don't tell me you and Ryan are having another baby."

"No. Nothing like that," I said, trying to figure out exactly how I was going to tell him that his brother was dead.

"Then what's up?"

"I don't really know how to tell you this." I paused, collecting my thoughts. "But back in January, Ryan got into a car accident on his way home from work one morning. He didn't survive."

Rick was silent on the other end. I worried that the connection broke. "Rick? Are you still there?"

"Yeah, I'm still here. I just, I don't think I heard you right."

"I'm so sorry, Rick."

"I can't believe it." I couldn't see his face, but by the sound of his voice, I could tell he was shocked. "Ryan's gone?"

"I wanted to let you know back in January when it happened. I tried calling you. I even looked for you on Facebook, but I couldn't find your account."

"I took it down before I left for Thailand." He paused for a moment before continuing. "Holy shit. I can't believe I missed my own brother's funeral."

I didn't bother telling him that there hadn't really been much of a funeral. I wondered if I would've done things differently if I had been able to reach Rick after his brother died. Maybe he could've handled Ryan's final arrangements instead. Although I doubted that would've happened. Rick could barely manage his own life, much less plan a funeral.

"How are you and the kids doing?"

"We're hanging in there. Jacob and Lydia miss their dad, but they're healing. It's been a little over six months. You know how kids are. They're pretty resilient."

"I miss those little guys."

"They're not so little anymore." I didn't really see how Rick could honestly claim he missed my kids since he'd only seen them a few times. He didn't call or send them cards on their birthdays or Christmas. It had been so long since he'd visited that I wasn't sure they even remembered him.

"I'd like to see them if that's okay with you."

"Where are you right now?"

"San Francisco. I'll be here for the next few days. Then I'm flying back to Texas," he said. "I can drive up to Sacramento first thing in the morning. You guys still live in the same house, right?"

"How long are you planning on visiting?" I asked, hoping it wouldn't be for long. I didn't know how I felt about Rick spending the night. I'd never had a comfortable relationship with him.

"Not long. I just want to say hi to Jack and Lydia and pay my respects to my brother. That's all I'm asking."

"It's Jacob," I corrected him. "Not Jack."

"That's what I meant."

Every fiber in my body told me this was a bad idea, but how could I tell Rick that I didn't think him visiting his niece and nephew was a good idea? "What were you doing in Thailand?" I asked, changing the subject.

"It sounds cheesy, but I went there to find myself."

With what money?

"The last time I talked to Ryan, we got into a huge argument. He told me I needed to get my shit together. So that's what I decided to do. I sold my motorcycle and my car, and I bought myself a ticket to the farthest place I could think of. Living there for the past eight months was a huge wake-up call."

"So you're back for good now?"

"Yup. I'm ready to get my life back on track."

The word "no" was still on the tip of my tongue, but I just couldn't bring myself to say it. "The kids are in summer camp for most of the day," I said, hoping to convince him that it wasn't worth it to drive all the way to Sacramento.

"I don't mind waiting for them to get home. Maybe we could grab dinner somewhere."

"Sure, okay," I said, wanting to kick myself the minute those words came out of my mouth. Something told me I was going to regret this visit big-time.

"Can you text me your address?"

"All right," I said. "But I've really got to get going, Rick. I've got a lot of work to do."

"Okay, I understand. I'll see you tomorrow."

I hung up, feeling completely awful for how insensitive I was being. I'd had months to adjust to the fact that Ryan was dead. For Rick, the news was completely new and, I imagined, a huge shock. I should've been more sympathetic, but I'd never particularly liked Rick. Everything he did came with an ulterior motive. I wondered if his visit would too. Maybe this time it would be different. Maybe he really had "found himself" on that trip he'd taken to Thailand.

Rick was such an unreliable person that when he arrived the following afternoon, I found myself surprised that he'd actually shown up. "Sorry I'm so late. Traffic in the Bay Area was a nightmare." He greeted me with a hug. "How are you doing?"

I managed a weak smile. "I've had almost six months to adjust, so I'm doing okay."

I led him inside and offered him something to drink. Standing next to him gave me the weirdest sense of déjà vu. He looked just a bit too much like Ryan for my comfort. A storm of bad memories flooded my mind. Rick had only just showed up, and I couldn't wait for his visit to come to an end.

I glanced at my phone, checking the time.

"The kids will be done with camp soon," I said. "I need to go pick them up. If you're thirsty, feel free to help yourself to something to drink."

"I can go with you."

"No, that's okay. I didn't tell Jacob or Lydia that you were coming yet. It's probably better if I give them a heads up."

I grabbed my car keys and bolted out of the house before Rick could say another word.

On the way back home from camp, I asked Jacob if he remembered his uncle Rick. I knew there was no way Lydia did.

"Not really," Jacob said, "Maybe a little."

"Well, he's your dad's brother, and he's at our house, waiting to see you guys."

"You mean right now?" Lydia asked.

"Yes. Right now."

"What's he like?" Jacob asked.

I wasn't sure how to answer that. "He looks a lot like your dad did."

"How long is he visiting?"

"Just for a few hours. He lives in Texas, and he's got to get back home soon, but he really wanted to see you guys before he left."

"Does he know about what happened to Daddy?" Lydia asked.

Jacob rolled his eyes. "Of course he does. Do you really think Mommy didn't tell him?"

"Well, I don't know," Lydia said defensively. "It was just a question."

"That's enough, you two," I said wearily. "No fighting please."

When we got home, I found Rick sitting at the table. He'd helped himself to some ice cream. As the kids took off their shoes, he got up and walked over to us.

"You must be Jacob and Lydia," he said, kneeling down in front of them. "I'm your uncle Rick."

Neither of my kids knew what to say. He was a total stranger to them, and they didn't do well around strangers.

"They're a little shy," I said, putting my hand on Jacob's shoulder. "Why don't I get you and your sister both a scoop of ice cream, and you can sit and eat it with your uncle Rick?"

"Um, okay," Jacob said.

While I filled two bowls with ice cream, the three of them sat down.

"So what kind of camp are you two going to?" Rick asked.

"Zoo camp," Lydia replied.

"Is it fun?"

"Yeah," Jacob said. "Kind of."

"It's not as much fun as hanging out with Mommy and Alex," Lydia chimed in.

"Who's Alex?" Rick asked.

"Mommy's boyfriend," Lydia replied before I could stop her. I'd forgotten to tell them not to mention Alex in front of Rick.

Rick turned to look at me. "You have a boyfriend already?" he asked, his voice accusatory.

My face heated. "Not that it's any of your business, but yes, I do."

"How long have you been dating him?"

"Like I said, it's not any of your business."

Rick stood up from the table and glared at me, reminding me even more of Ryan than when he'd first shown up. "That's fucked up, Vanessa."

My kids' eyes widened. They weren't used to hearing profanity. "Jacob, Lydia. I need you two to go to your room right now. Mommy and Rick need to have a private conversation."

Neither of them argued with me. Instead, they got up from the table and hustled silently down the hallway.

"My brother hasn't even been dead for a year, and you've already moved on. I can't believe you."

My pulse raced, ready for a fight. I'd been through years of this with Ryan. I was not about to let Rick treat me the way his brother had. "You know what I can't believe?" I said, "That you decide to show up here out of the blue after doing God knows what halfway around the world and think you have the right to an opinion about what I do or how I live my life. You never gave a crap about your brother when he was alive. The only time you called Ryan was when you needed something from him."

"I might not have come around much, but at least I loved my brother. Unlike you."

"You don't know what you're talking about."

"Ryan told me how hard he tried to make you happy. That no matter how much he did for you, it was never enough."

Of course he had. I shook my head and took a deep breath, trying to keep my temper in check. "There's two sides to every story."

"You hooking up with some guy so soon after my brother died tells me everything I need to know."

My face flushed. I bit back the angry tears I felt forming in my eyes. "I don't care what you think. It's been years since I've seen you or talked to you. Jacob, your one and only nephew, barely even remembers who you are. As far as I'm concerned, we're better off without you in our lives."

"At least I cared about my brother. It's obvious you didn't give a fuck about him."

I pointed to the door. "Get out of my house. Now."

"This was my brother's house."

"Well, he's dead, so it's my house now, and I don't want you in it."

He glared at me. "Fine, I'll go. But at least tell me where you buried my brother. I want to visit his grave before I go back to Texas."

"I didn't bury him. His body was cremated."

His eyes widened. "You heartless bitch. I can't believe you didn't give my brother a proper burial."

His words were like a slap in my face. But I refused to give him the satisfaction of thinking that he'd gotten to me. "A lot of people get cremated these days," I said. "And for your information, I tried reaching you after Ryan died to ask about his final arrangements, but you were nowhere to be found. That meant I had to decide."

Rick stared at me, incredulous. He looked over his shoulder at the fireplace, searching for an urn.

"What did you do with his ashes?"

"I scattered them," I said simply.

"Where?"

"In a park we used to take the kids to together."

Rick opened his mouth to say something then closed it. Unfortunately, he didn't remain speechless for long. "So instead of burying my brother in a cemetery, you have his body burned, and then you throw his ashes away. What kind of person does that?"

"I didn't throw them away. I scattered them. Lots of people do that."

"Did you even bother to think about how I'd feel about it?"

"Like I said, I tried to reach you—"

"Did my brother leave anything for me?" Rick asked cutting me off and abruptly changing the subject.

"Anything like what?"

"I don't know, like maybe a letter or some personal items ... or money."

I gritted my teeth. This was the purpose of Rick's visit all along. I doubted he cared less about seeing his niece and nephew. He'd only insisted on a visit because he hoped Ryan had left behind a stash of money for him. "No, he didn't."

"I'm his brother. His *only* brother. I can't believe he wouldn't leave anything for me."

"He left everything to me because we have two kids. Kids that need a house and food and clothes and hopefully college tuition one day. You're a grown man who can take care of himself."

"I don't believe you."

"And I want you to leave. Now!"

I walked over to the front door and held it open.

"This isn't over," Rick grumbled as he walked outside. "I'm calling a lawyer. I want my share of Ryan's assets, and you're not going to stop me from getting them."

"Go ahead. I'd like to see you try."

Rick had no leg to stand on when it came to Ryan's inheritance. I didn't need a law degree to know that. Sooner or later he'd figure that out, and then he'd leave me the hell alone. For good. I slammed the door shut, pressed my back against it, and took a few deep breaths to calm myself down.

A few minutes later, Jacob and Lydia crept down the hallway.

"Where's Rick?" Jacob asked.

"He's gone."

"Good," Lydia said. "I don't like him. He's not very nice."

"He kind of reminded me of Dad," Jacob added.

"Why was he so mad anyway?" Lydia asked.

"I don't want to talk about it." I ran a shaky hand through my hair. "I'm sorry you had to hear us fighting."

"It's okay, Mommy," Lydia said, giving me a hug. It made me feel better, but I was still angry long after the kids went to bed. I was too upset to sleep and wound up spending most of the night tossing and turning in bed. Rick and Ryan's last words to me got all jumbled up in my head and I couldn't shake the awful feeling in the pit of my stomach.

ONCE MORNING CAME I'd take the kids to camp, go to the gym and blow off some steam on the treadmill, and then I'd tell Alex all about Rick's visit. He'd find a way to make me feel better. Even though I felt lower than low right now, I told myself that in a few days, my dead husband's asshole brother and the horrible things he'd said to me would be forgotten.

20

I didn't wind up telling Alex about Rick. He was so excited the next day about the good news his lawyer had shared with him the night before that I didn't want to ruin his exuberant mood. She'd filed the papers needed to get a date for a custody trial set, and in the meantime, the judge had granted him temporary visitation privileges with his daughter so his ex-wife had no choice but to let Alex have time with Leah.

"I'm so happy for you," I said, pushing Rick and all the ugly things he'd said to me the day before to the back of my mind.

"I want you and your kids to meet Leah. Maybe not this weekend, but soon. What do you think?"

"Of course we want to meet her."

"I'm nervous about what her mother's going to tell her," he said. "Who knows what garbage Kristi's been filling Leah's head with."

"Now that you get to see Leah, you can tell her your side of things."

"Yeah, I know, but I don't want her to feel like a ping-pong ball. She shouldn't have to pick sides."

"Try not to worry," I said, taking his hand.

He smiled, but I knew underneath it he was worried. Ever since he'd hired a lawyer to help him gain joint custody, he went back and forth between excitement at the prospect of getting more time with Leah and anxiety over her finding out the truth.

I didn't want to place another burden on Alex's shoulders, so I kept my mouth shut about Rick's short but disastrous visit. Instead, I talked to Marla and Lynette about it.

"He sounds a lot like Ryan," Marla muttered. "Which explains his temper. It must be a family trait."

"I hope not. The last thing I want is for either Jacob or Lydia to act like that when they grow up."

"They won't, because they have you teaching them the right way to behave," Marla said.

"You aren't letting what Rick said get to you, are you?" Lynette asked. "He sounds like a total asshole."

"I don't know. I'm trying not to. But it's hard. Over the past few months, I've slowly stopped beating myself up about everything that went wrong between me and Ryan and the way I felt after he died, but Rick's visit brought it all back. I can't stop feeling guilty about everything all the time."

"You have nothing to feel guilty about," Marla insisted.

"You're wrong," I whispered, too ashamed to say the words any louder. There were things Marla and Lynette didn't know, things I couldn't bring myself to tell them.

"I still can't believe he had the nerve to curse at you in front of the kids," Lynette said.

"Can we talk about something else?" I was the one who'd brought Rick up, but our conversation was starting to make me feel ill. Normally, venting to my friends helped, but talking about Ryan and his brother was only making me feel worse.

Long after Marla and Lynette went home, my somber mood persisted. I tried willing the awful feeling inside me away, but it refused to budge. That voice felt like it was screaming at me.

Around the kids, I managed to mostly hold myself together, but at night I struggled to sleep. I kept thinking about all the things I could've done differently. My insomnia had returned with a vengeance.

I didn't want Alex to know. He was happier than I'd ever seen him. Especially after the weekend he'd spent with his daughter. That Monday, Leah was all he could talk about.

"I told her all about you," he said.

"She wasn't upset that you have a girlfriend?"

"No. She's actually excited to meet you," he said. "I get her the weekend after next. We should have lunch and then hang out at my place after. Have your kids bring their swimsuits. We can have a family pool party."

"They'd love that." And so would I. But as much fun as it sounded, I couldn't stop the alarm bells from going off in my head. I kept hearing Rick telling me how fucked up I was. Maybe he was right about me, and Alex was wrong. Would Leah see through me? I didn't want to come between her and her father.

Later that day, when I told the kids about Alex's invitation, they were thrilled, just like I knew they'd be. We didn't have a pool at my house. In Sacramento, summer temperatures often soared to over a hundred degrees. When it got that hot, there wasn't much you could do outside except swim, so the kids got super excited whenever anyone with a pool invited them over. They'd already swum at Alex's a few times and frequently asked when they'd get to again.

Despite the storm brewing inside me, I was also excited. I couldn't help but wonder what Leah was like. I hoped that she and my kids would get along. I wanted this to work more than anything. My kids were already so emotionally invested in Alex that I couldn't stomach the idea of anything going wrong.

ON THE DAY we were to meet Alex's daughter, I got up early to pack the kids' bathing suits and towels for later. I also picked out their clothes even though they really were old enough to do that on their own. But sometimes those clothes didn't exactly match, or they chose a shirt with stains on it that had somehow got past my radar when I did laundry. I doubted Leah would care what my kids wore, but keeping my hands busy helped occupy my mind.

By noon, we were all dressed and ready to go. We met Alex in front of a pizza restaurant in Midtown. He greeted me with a kiss on the cheek and the kids with hugs.

"Have you been waiting long?" I asked.

"No, we just got here."

I smiled at the girl beside him and held out my hand. "You must be Leah. I'm Vanessa. It's so nice to meet you."

"Nice to meet you too," she said, shaking my hand.

"These are my kids, Jacob and Lydia."

She glanced at them and gave a sheepish wave. "Hi."

They replied with "hi," nervously fidgeting at the same time. Our kids had at least one thing in common.

"Who's hungry for pizza?" Alex asked, trying to break up the awkward silence.

"I am," Lydia replied excitedly. She turned to me and pulled on my shirt. "Can you ask them to give us some dough balls to play with?"

"Sure," I said as Alex held the door open for us.

We were seated, and a few minutes later, a waiter came by with water and three small globs of pizza dough. I hadn't even needed to ask for it. The kids eagerly took it from him and got busy playing.

"This pizza dough thing really is genius," Alex whispered to me.

"I know." Not only was it keeping the three kids busy, but

they were interacting, showing each other different things they could make with the dough. I glanced up from my menu, studying Leah while trying not to be too obvious about it. She looked so little like Alex that I understood why he'd suspected she wasn't his biological daughter even before his ex confessed her infidelity. Leah had rust-colored hair and brown eyes. But it wasn't just their coloring that was different. Her features were nothing like Alex's. Her jaw was soft, his was angled. She had a high forehead while his was rather short.

By the time the kids' pizza arrived, they were all smiles, and I'd even heard them laugh a few times. They were in mutual agreement that the best pizza had only two things on it: tomato sauce and cheese. They even agreed to share, instead of each of them asking for their own pie. Alex and I both glanced at each other out of the corners of our eyes. I could tell he was thinking the same thing I was. We were both pleased at how well everyone was getting along.

"Who's excited about going to the pool after lunch?" Alex asked.

"Me," they all said in unison.

"Are you a good swimmer?" I asked Leah, trying to pull her into conversation.

"Kind of," she said.

"Leah was on the swim team for a few years," Alex said.

"Oh really? What was your favorite stroke?"

"Back stroke. Or breast stroke. I don't know. I like them both."

"Well, you'll have to show Jacob and Lydia later. They only know freestyle."

"What's freestyle?" Lydia asked.

"It's regular swimming," Jacob said.

"If it's regular swimming, why don't they just call it that? Why do they have to call it freestyle?"

Leah started laughing. The three of them got into a spirited debate about swim strokes while they finished their pizza. For dessert, they all got a scoop of gelato. By the time they were finished with it, they were beyond excited to get over to Alex's house and into his pool. At just after one in the afternoon, it was blazingly hot out. It would stay that way for another three months. Sunny, hot, no rain or clouds. The weather in California's north valley was boringly predictable, but I supposed that was better than a surprise rainstorm ruining carefully laid plans.

The kids changed into their swimsuits as soon as we got to Alex's house. They ran outside to the backyard and screamed as they did their first cannonballs into his pool. Alex and I sat beside each other on patio chairs under the shade of an awning.

"They seem to be getting along really well," Alex said.

"Yeah. Even better than I thought they would."

I leaned back in the chair and looked at the kids. They were trying to sort out how they could do a cannonball all at the same time. I loved how happy the three of them looked. Nothing made me feel more at peace than watching my children wear genuine smiles on their faces. I knew Alex felt the same way. Which was why he worried endlessly about what his ex would do. She carried the truth about Alex not being Leah's biological dad like a grenade, and no one knew when she was going to pull the pin out.

"Have you spoken to your ex at all since you petitioned for custody?" I asked, hoping that he'd found a way to get her to see that there was a right way and a wrong way to tell a child life-altering information.

"My lawyer advised me to avoid getting into any conflicts with Kristi, so the only time I speak to her is when I pick Leah up and drop her off. And even then, it's mostly just hi and bye. Her lawyer must've told her the same thing because she hasn't said much to me. But I can tell she's pissed. I can see it in her eyes."

I turned my head from Alex to look at the pool. Leah was showing Jacob and Lydia how to backstroke. "Has there been any news from your lawyer?"

"Nothing. I'm still waiting to hear when the trial date will be set. All Linda has said is that I need to be on my best behavior so the judge will have a good opinion of me."

Alex wouldn't have any trouble with that. Even in high school he'd been one of the good guys. He rarely cursed. He got decent grades, and he didn't mess around with alcohol or drugs like so many of our classmates had. Not much had changed. He maybe had an occasional beer when we went out to eat, but that was about it. "You're Leah's father. Even if you don't share the same DNA. You raised her. You've been making child support payments every month. You have a right to joint custody."

"Yeah, but I messed up when I agreed to give Kristi primary custody after the divorce. I'm going to have to prove to the judge that I deserve joint custody."

"You're worried, aren't you?" I didn't need to ask the question. I could hear it in his voice.

"As long as Kristi doesn't find some bullshit dirt to use against me, I should be fine."

I squeezed Alex's hand, wishing that I could do more to reassure him. After another few minutes, the kids got out of the pool, ready for a little break. Leah walked over to her dad and gave him a big hug. He smiled, not seeming to care that she'd got him all wet. They appeared to have a close relationship. She was a daddy's girl. It wasn't a concept I was really familiar with since my own dad had left when I was still so young, and Ryan's temper made Lydia fear him more often than not. I deeply regretted that. When I'd married Ryan, I hadn't really thought about the fact that I was not only choosing a husband for myself but a father for my children. Whenever one of the kids came crying to me after he'd yelled at them, I felt terrible that I'd chosen wrong.

Once my mind got started on a train of thought, it was hard for me to change course. Even after the kids got back in the pool, I continued to sit there thinking.

"Is something wrong?" Alex asked.

"No." I managed a smile. "I've just got a few things on my mind."

Alex raised his brow. "What kind of things?"

I couldn't bring myself to tell him. "Nothing," I said. "It's not important."

"You know you can tell me anything, right?"

I nodded. I *could* tell him anything, but there was just so much I *couldn't* bring myself to say.

"How about we get these kids some ice cream?" Alex asked, getting up from his chair. "I've got chocolate and cookies and cream in my freezer."

"They just had gelato at lunch."

"Yeah, but did you see how small those bowls were? Plus, I'm starting to get really hot, and I don't think the kids are going to let us get away with eating ice cream in front of them."

"You have a point," I agreed."Bring some bowls and spoons, and I'll help you scoop."

After their ice cream break, the kids went right back into the pool. They were having so much fun that I wasn't able to pry them away until close to dinnertime. It took me telling them, "five more minutes" at least three times before they grudgingly changed back into their dry clothes.

While they were in the bathroom, I walked over to Leah. "It was really nice to meet you. Hopefully, we'll get to see you again soon."

"We'd like that." Alex put his hands on his daughter's shoulders. She looked up at him adoringly. "Right, Leah?"

"Yeah."

The kids finished up in the bathroom and handed me their wet towels and bathing suits. "Go tell Alex and Leah thank you," I instructed them.

They said their goodbyes, and then I loaded them into the car. A few minutes after I arrived home, Alex texted.

I think things went really well, don't you?

Yes. Leah is such a sweet girl. I'm glad I got to meet her.

And I really was. I'd had a great afternoon, and so had the kids. I could picture it in my mind. Alex and me, his kids and mine. The images were beautiful, heartwarming, but the ugly voice in my head that interrupted wasn't. Ever since Rick's visit, it had gotten a million times louder.

What are you doing? You don't deserve a man like Alex. If he knew who you really were, he wouldn't want you. I managed to drown the voice out by watching a movie with the kids, but when I went to bed later that night, it returned with a ferociousness I hadn't seen coming. And I couldn't help but wonder if maybe the voice was right. Alex had a custody battle coming up. Every aspect of his life would be scrutinized. What if I wound up being the bullshit dirt Kristi's lawyer used against Alex? All he'd need to do was track down Rick. I was sure my former brother-in-law would be more than happy to give Kristi's lawyer an earful about what a terrible person I was. Lawyers were good at twisting things. What if Kristi's made it look like I'd be a bad influence on her daughter? I didn't want to be the reason Alex lost Leah. I already had enough guilt to live with.

On Monday, I woke up tired and miserable. I decided to skip the gym. I hadn't slept well the night before, and sometime over those sleepless hours, I'd made a decision. Until Alex's custody case was over, and maybe even after that, I needed to give him space. I tried not to think about how unhappy it would make me or possibly even Alex, who seemed to have no idea how toxic I really was.

With the kids' camp over, I had them home with me for the entire day. It made getting work done nearly impossible. I racked my brain, trying to come up with fun activities for them, but everything I thought of involved more energy than I could muster.

By Wednesday morning, when I backed out of going to the gym again by text message, Alex called, demanding to know what was going on.

"Nothing," I insisted.

"You never miss this many days at the gym. Unless you're mad at me. Did I do something wrong?"

"No. It's not like that at all."

"Then does that mean I'll get to see you tomorrow?"

I couldn't think of a reason to back out again. At least not one that I could explain over the phone. "Yeah. I'll be there."

I hung up the phone feeling miserable. Usually I was good at hiding my melancholy moods from the kids, but Jacob noticed something was wrong.

"Are you getting sick, Mommy?"

"No. Why do you ask?"

"You haven't gotten up from the couch all day."

"Mommy's just tired. That's all," I said, managing a smile. "The heat's been sucking up all my energy."

I decided to call Marla. She was just as desperate as I was to keep her kids busy. We decided to meet at the frozen yogurt place across the street. That short of a walk I could still manage.

"How much longer is summer vacation?" Marla asked as we sat down.

"A month and a half," I said. "I wouldn't mind if I had enough money to take time off work and bring the kids somewhere fun, but I don't."

"You look tired," Marla said, scrutinizing my appearance. "Is everything okay?"

I shook my head. "I haven't been sleeping well. Not since Rick's visit."

"Don't tell me you're still letting what that jerk said get to you."

I stared down at my feet and bit my lower lip. I'd been fighting back tears ever since Rick had stormed out of my house, not wanting the kids or Alex to see me cry. And my lack of sleep wasn't helping things. It wasn't just what Rick had said that had me so upset, I'd struggled with my emotions for months after Ryan died, but I'd been getting a handle on them, until Rick's visit. His words had pushed me ten steps backward. "I can't help it."

"What's Alex got to say about all this?"

I lifted my gaze. "I never told him about Rick's visit."

Marla frowned. "Why not? He's your boyfriend. His job is to make you feel better."

I thought about just keeping my mouth shut since I knew exactly how Marla would respond to what I was about to say, but I decided to tell her anyway. "Alex is in the middle of a custody battle. The last thing he needs to deal with are my problems."

"I know he wouldn't see it that way."

"Yeah, he wouldn't. Which means it's my job to look out for him."

Marla lifted her head to look over my shoulder. "Abby," she shouted. "Let go of your brother's hand."

I turned to see what was going on. Abby was squeezing her brother's wrist so hard she was leaving crescent-shaped fingernail marks on his skin.

"He just stuck his hand in my frozen yogurt."

Marla got up to pull her kids apart. "That doesn't mean you have to rip his skin off."

She proceeded to give her two oldest kids a lecture about two wrongs not making a right then sat back down next to me. "Sheesh, I can't even enjoy a frozen yogurt without them at each other's throats. What's your secret? Jacob and Lydia are so tame compared to my wild animals."

I laughed. "Maybe in front of you they are, but believe me, they get into it plenty."

Marla didn't bring Alex up again. Thankfully, the little disagreement her kids got into was enough of a distraction that she forgot what we'd been talking about. Instead, she started telling me about some guy she'd given her number to. His kids went to the same school as ours. "Turns out his wife cheated on him, too, so we've got that in common."

"I'm not sure if that's a good thing or a bad thing."

"Neither am I. I'm already picturing our first date. We'll be sitting there, trash-talking our exes over sushi and green tea."

"You'll be able to empathize with each other," I said. "That's not a bad thing."

She shrugged. "I suppose."

WHEN MORNING CAME, I let the kids know I was bringing them to Kids Club. They liked going because there were lots of fun activities for them to do. I should've been bringing them all week so they could catch a break from cartoons and video games and play with other kids instead of just each other. Thinking that only made me feel worse than I already did. After Ryan died, I'd sworn I could do this single-mother thing. Now I doubted everything. Especially myself. As soon as Jacob and Lydia saw Alex waiting for me in the lobby, they ran toward him. Lydia threw her arms around Alex.

"We didn't know you were going to be here," Jacob said.

My kids were already so attached to him. I began to second-guess myself again. But then I reminded myself that in the long term it would be harder for everyone involved if Alex and I imploded somewhere down the line. It would be easier if we parted ways now before our lives became further intertwined.

We barely talked that morning. I was too distracted by my thoughts. Alex sensed something was off with me. Twice he'd asked what was wrong. Both times I'd said, "Nothing."

By the expression on Alex's face, I could tell he didn't believe me.

When we were done working out, Alex insisted on coming with me to sign Jacob and Lydia out from Kids Club. "It's okay," I told him. "I know you have to get to work."

He frowned. "Will I see you tomorrow?"

I couldn't bring myself to say no. Instead, I nodded. Alex

leaned forward to give me a kiss. I turned my head, giving him my cheek. I watched as he walked away, torn between wanting him and feeling like I didn't deserve the happiness he brought me. Maybe raising Jacob and Lydia on my own and letting Alex go so he could win his custody case and move on with someone better was my penance. My chance to make up for failing Ryan. I just needed to find a way to make Alex understand that.

The next day, Alex pressed me again to tell him what was bothering me, but I couldn't bring myself to say the words out loud.

"It's nothing. I've just got a lot on my mind. The kids' camp is over. I've got to figure out how to keep them busy while at the same time keep my job."

"I could probably take a few days off work. I'd love to hang out with Jacob and Lydia."

Of course he'd offer that kind of thing. "You don't need to do that."

"I don't like seeing you so stressed out." He put his hand on the middle of my back. My heart did a backflip. I missed his touch. It had been so long, too long, since we'd gotten to kiss, to hold, or to love each other. I missed it terribly.

I managed a smile. "I'll be okay."

All the next day, I let Alex's calls go to voice mail and didn't reply to his texts except to say I'd be busy all weekend running around with the kids. I'd slipped into such a funk that I didn't even have the energy to get dressed until close to noon. I took the kids to a movie and stuffed my face with popcorn and candy, but nothing seemed to fill the hole inside of me. If anything, it felt like it was getting bigger and bigger every day.

THE NEXT MORNING, after throwing a load of the kids' clothes into the washing machine and turning it on, I saw water dripping from the bottom of the washing machine's door.

"Crap." This was the last thing I needed. I inspected the machine and found where the leak was coming from, but it wasn't anything I knew how to fix.

I called Marla. "Any chance you know how to fix a washing machine?" I asked.

"Um, no. And even if I did, I'm not home right now," she said.

I cursed under my breath.

"Why don't you call Alex? Isn't he pretty handy? I bet he knows how to fix things like that."

She was right. Alex would know. But I didn't want to have to ask him for help. I stared at the overflowing laundry basket. I had several more loads just like it that I needed to get done and knew there would be no service center open on a Sunday to fix my leaky washing machine.

"Yeah, I guess I'll do that."

Instead of calling Alex, I made breakfast. Eventually, I'd have to figure out what to do about the piles of dirty clothes, but I'd think about that later. The kids had a birthday party to go to in another few hours. When they were gone, I'd fiddle around with the washing machine and figure something out.

Nothing I did worked. What I needed was a new part, but even if I ran to the hardware store, I wouldn't know how to replace it.

With a deep sigh, I gave up and decided to text Alex.

Any chance you can come over and give me hand? My washing machine has sprung a leak.

He replied right away.

I'll be right over.

Alex figured out what the problem was in less than a minute. Turned out I was right. I did need a new part.

"Can I get it at the hardware store?" I asked.

"No. You'd need to go to an appliance parts center."

I sighed and ran a hand through my messy hair. "Great, just what I need."

"Luckily," he said, "I happen to know a place, and they're open on Sundays."

"Oh my God, you're a lifesaver." I almost threw my arms around him but stopped myself.

"But I'm not going until you tell me what the hell is going on with you."

I crossed my arms. "I don't know what you're talking about."

"You told me you'd be busy with Jacob and Lydia, but they're not even here, so that was obviously an excuse to get out of seeing me. What I don't get is why."

I leaned against the wall, trying not to stare at Alex. He was wearing jeans and a fitted T-shirt that showed off his well-sculpted torso. It seemed like forever since those arms of his had been wrapped around me. I wanted him to pick me up, carry me to the bedroom, and make passionate love to me.

"I ... I don't know what you're talking about." I felt like the world's biggest coward. Why couldn't I just tell him the truth? That I was no good for him. I'd known it since the beginning. That was the real reason I was so scared to get involved with him. I didn't want to ruin his life like I had Ryan's. If I'd been strong enough to tell Ryan that we weren't right for each other, maybe he'd have eventually found someone who could've made him happy, and maybe he'd still be alive. The thought sent a chill through me.

Alex reached for my arms, uncrossed them, and held my hands in his. "You've been giving me the silent treatment all week. Don't think I haven't noticed."

I looked away and pulled my hands from his grasp.

"I thought we had a great time last Saturday," he continued, "but ever since then, you've been shutting me out. Is it because of Leah?"

"No. Of course not. She's an amazing girl."

"Then what is it?"

I took a deep breath. "I know you're not going to like this, but I think that maybe we should take a break from each other."

His jaw twitched, and his eyes narrowed. He stared at me for a moment as if he was trying to figure out if I meant what I'd just said. "I ... I don't want to take a break," Alex said, his voice hard. "There's no reason to."

"You're in the middle of a custody case. I don't want to be the reason you lose your daughter."

He furrowed his brows. "Why would you be the reason I lost Leah?"

Your ex will dig up every piece of dirt on you that she can find to keep you away from Leah.

"It's not like you're a drug dealer or a child abuser. You're a better mom than Kristi ever was or will be."

Tears started to form. I stared down at my feet, not wanting Alex to see them. "You only say that because there's things you don't know."

"Things?" He seemed to be getting angrier by the moment. "What things?"

I lifted my head, meeting his gaze. "I'm not the same person I was in high school. I wish I was, but I'm not, and it's finally time I stopped pretending."

"What's that supposed to mean?"

"I've changed," I said, trying to keep my voice from cracking. "I met someone I thought I loved, and I got married, and I thought I would live happily ever after. We had two beautiful kids, a house. The American dream."

"And from everything you told me, he was a shitty guy." Alex furrowed his brows again. "Is that what this is about? Despite what he put you through, you miss him. You barely had a chance to grieve, and then I came along demanding that you give me a chance."

I couldn't stand it for a minute longer. Why couldn't he just see? Why was he forcing me to confess my sins out loud? I stormed out of the laundry room.

He followed and grabbed my hand. I whirled around to face him. "Don't make me do this."

"Do what?" he asked, still obviously confused.

I had no choice but to tell him. It was the only way to get him to see that in the end I'd make his life miserable. I stared into his eyes steeling myself for what I was about to reveal. "I'm not grieving over Ryan. I've never grieved for him. Because I didn't love him. Actually, I more than didn't love him. Sometimes I downright hated his guts."

Alex narrowed his eyes at me again. "If Ryan isn't the problem, then what is?"

"Don't you get it?" I threw my hands up in frustration. "*I'm* the problem."

"How are you the problem? What am I not seeing?"

"That I'm a terrible person."

"No. You're not."

I shook my head. He obviously didn't understand what I was trying to tell him. I didn't want to have to draw a picture for him, but he was giving me no choice. "You're wrong about me. If I wasn't a terrible person, then I wouldn't have been happy when I found out my husband died. But guess what? I was. I was glad I'd never have to answer to him again or have another fight with him. I was glad that he'd never touch me again, that I didn't have to share my bed with him. What kind of person feels that way?" Tears streamed down my face. I wrapped my arms around myself, suddenly cold even though it was almost triple digits outside.

"Someone whose husband treated her like garbage," Alex said. The gentleness in his voice made me feel even worse. I didn't deserve his pity.

"What if your ex finds out how soon you and I got together after Ryan died? What if her lawyer tracks down Ryan's brother? He hates me you know, and he's got plenty bad to say about me. The judge will see what a terrible person I am. He won't want Leah around me. I know you think you want to be with me, but you won't feel that way if I'm the reason you never get to see your daughter again."

Alex took a step closer to me. He tried to reach for me, but I backed away. "Vanessa, if the judge turns down my request for joint custody, it will be because I screwed things up, not because of you."

"I don't want to mess things up for you."

"Then stop doing this. Stop thinking what you're thinking, and tell me that you've changed you mind about all of this "we need some space" bullshit. Because I can't do this without you. I can't fight for Leah if you're not by my side. You're the one who gave me the courage and the strength to find a lawyer and ask for custody in the first place."

"You don't need me. You only think you do."

Alex took another step closer. I backed away again, this time right into the chair of my dining table, giving Alex the moment he was looking for. He wrapped me in his arms. They were warm and strong and comforting and robbed me of all my resolve. Just like he had in the parking lot of the gym when he first told me he had feelings for me. Deep down I'd known then, just like I did now, that I was no good for him, but I'd refused to admit the truth to myself. If it wasn't for Leah, maybe I never would have.

"I love you, Vanessa. You're the best thing that's ever

happened to me. I'm not letting you walk away from me without a fight."

"Oh, Alex. I'm no good for you. I'll ruin your life just like I ruined Ryan's."

"From where I stand, he's the one who did all the ruining."

"Because you haven't heard his side of the story. If you had, he'd tell you I didn't love him enough, that I never paid attention to him, that I only loved the kids and not him. He'd tell you that I poisoned their minds and made them hate him. I made him so unhappy."

"He'd tell me those things because he was a selfish asshole."

"That's not what his brother thinks."

Alex took a step back and stared at me. "His brother? What does he have to do with any of this?"

I hadn't planned on telling Alex about Rick's visit, but since I'd brought it up, I couldn't very well take my words back. I explained how Lydia had accidentally let it slip that I had a boyfriend and the way Rick had responded to the news.

"He sounds like he's just as much of an asshole as Ryan was," Alex said. He frowned. "Why am I only hearing about this now?"

"I was going to tell you, but you were so happy about getting visitation with Leah that I didn't want to bring you down with some sob story about how my brother-in-law decided to drop in and tell me I'm the worst wife and mother on the planet."

"Sounds like he was just sore because Ryan didn't leave any money for him."

I shook my head. "There's something else," I said, my voice barely above a whisper. "Something I've never told anyone."

"What is it?"

I inhaled, bracing myself. I was so scared to say the words out loud, but I had no choice. I was dying inside. And Alex deserved to know the truth. He needed to know I wasn't the person he thought I was. "The day before Ryan died we had a terrible argument. He told me that he knew me and the kids didn't want him around. I think he was waiting for me to tell him that it wasn't true, but I didn't. I just kept quiet because I was so tired of arguing." I looked up at Alex, his eyes were full of sympathy. "He told me he was going to kill himself. He said we'd be happier with him out of our lives. I didn't take him seriously, though. I thought he was just trying to get a reaction out of me. It wasn't the first time he'd threatened to commit suicide. I never dreamed he actually meant it, but what if he did? What if his car accident wasn't really an accident? For all I know, he got into that car crash on purpose. What if I'm the reason he's dead?"

"Oh my God, Vanessa, you've got to stop thinking that way. Even if Ryan's death was a suicide, which I highly doubt, it's not your fault."

I turned my back to Alex. A part of me wanted to believe he was right, but guilt held so much power over me that I just couldn't let it go. It had tangled its ugly web through every cell in my body.

"I'm no good, Alex. Why can't I get you to see that?"

"I can't believe you've been living with this guilt for all these months without saying anything to anyone. I wish you would've told me sooner so I could've told you that you aren't to blame for Ryan's death. You aren't responsible for other people's happiness. It sounds like your husband had a lot of problems, problems that were his responsibility to get help for. Instead he wore you down and made you feel like everything that went wrong in your marriage was your fault. But it wasn't."

"I should've tried harder to help him."

"Stop saying that, Vanessa. You can't help someone who doesn't want to be helped."

I felt Alex inch closer. He put his hand on my waist, leaned in, and pressed his body against mine. He inhaled my scent. I felt myself get all tingly inside. Why did I have to want him as much as I did? A moment later he spun me around and kissed me. I stiffened, but as he deepened the kiss I relaxed, my body melting into his as he pulled me closer. I was emotionally drained. My heart hurt, and Alex made everything better. I had no fight left in me. Maybe after. After he made love to me, I'd find a way to get through to him.

He wiped my tears with his fingertips before trailing kisses down my neck. His hands wrapped themselves in my hair. I tried to stifle my moan, but it was no use. It had been too long since we'd touched like this, and his hands, his lips, were driving me wild. I pulled my shirt over my head then found his lips again. He cupped one of my breasts, and my breath hitched. Step by step we managed to stumble over to my bedroom, dropping pieces of clothing on the floor as we went. By the time Alex laid me down on the bed, I couldn't bring myself to tell him he was making a big mistake.

"We shouldn't have done that," I said after Alex had made love to me not once but twice.

He rolled over to his side and looked down at me. "Don't do this, Vanessa. You're beating yourself up about things that aren't your fault. You deserve to be happy. You just have to let yourself be."

I rested my hand on his cheek. "I want to believe that. I really do. I'm just not sure I know how."

"Because you don't see what I do. You see the person your husband convinced you that you are. And then you let that no-good brother of his get in your head. But they're both wrong."

If Alex believed in me as much as he said he did, then maybe some of his faith could rub off on me. I managed a weak smile. I wasn't quite yet ready to shake my fear that I'd somehow mess things up for him, but putting my thoughts into words earlier had somehow helped. For months I'd bottled up so many emotions, but now that they were out it was like a load had been lifted from my shoulders.

"I feel like I don't deserve this. I don't deserve you."

Alex stroked my cheek with his thumb. "Believe it or not, I

know what you're going through. After I found out Kristi had cheated on me, she somehow twisted things around and made me feel like it was my fault. For a while, I was convinced that if I'd been a better husband, she wouldn't have had to turn to other guys to make her happy."

"What made you change your mind?"

"My mom."

"Your mom?" I vaguely remembered her, but I didn't know her as well as I knew some of my other friends' mothers.

"My dad cheated on my mom too. When I was a kid, so I had no idea. They stayed together because of me, but as soon as I moved out of the house, my parents got a divorce. So my mom understood what I was going through. She said a betrayal like that leaves you traumatized. When you give your heart to someone and they break it, it's hard to just get over it. Ryan may not have cheated on you, but he abused you. Not with his fists, but with his words. You were his victim. And he managed to get you so twisted around that you blame yourself."

"Sometimes I see things that way, but then I feel bad. Like I'm only seeing it because I can't live with the guilt."

"Do you know what I see when I look at you?"

I shook my head.

"I see a beautiful woman who's been through a lot. A single mother who puts her kids ahead of herself." He twirled a lock of my hair with his fingers. "A woman who doesn't lie, and a woman who's made me believe in things I didn't think were possible."

"Oh really? Like what?"

"Like second chances." He gave me a kiss and then stared into my eyes. "We can heal each other, Vanessa."

I draped my arm around Alex. "I'd like that."

"What we have, it's good. I can't let it go. I won't let it go. Promise me you won't either."

I ignored the lingering doubts, pushing them out of my head. "I won't. I promise."

"And promise me that you won't keep things from me," he urged. "You should've told me a lot sooner about Rick and about what was going on inside that head of yours."

I gave him a weak smile. "You're right. I should have."

I glanced at my bedside clock. "Oh shit," I said. "I have to pick up the kids in fifteen minutes."

Alex got out of bed too. "I want to go with you."

"You don't need to do that."

Alex reached for my hand. I looked up at him. "I know I don't need to, but I want to. And besides, I miss Jacob and Lydia. And I'm pretty sure they miss me too."

He was right about that. They loved him.

"All right," I said. "But you better hurry up."

A few minutes later, I raced down the street on my way to Bounce High to pick up the kids. They were delighted to see Alex in the passenger seat.

"What are you doing here?" Lydia asked him.

"Just thought I'd surprise you guys."

"Did you have fun at the party?" I asked, glancing over my shoulder as the kids got into the car.

"Yeah," Jacob said. "It was super fun."

"Does that mean you're too tired to come over to my house and play in the pool?" Alex asked.

Jacob and Lydia bounced up and down in their seats. "Ooh, Mommy, can we, can we?"

"Um, sure, I guess so," I replied. "When we get home, go ahead and grab your towels and bathing suits."

The kids were so excited that they ran into the house as soon as I parked in the driveway. While Alex and I waited for them to get their swim stuff together, he turned to me. "I have a great idea."

I smiled. "Another one?"

"Yup." He reached for my hand, lacing his fingers through mine. "How about you three spend the night?"

I opened my mouth to answer, but I wasn't really sure what to say. It seemed like such a big step.

"Before you say no, hear me out—"

"I'm not going to say no," I said, smiling. "I was going to tell you I still have a washing machine that needs fixing."

"You can bring your laundry to my place."

It suddenly dawned on me that nothing would make me happier than to wake up next to Alex in the morning. I knew the kids wouldn't mind. If anything, they'd be excited. They told me all the time how much cooler Alex's house was than ours, and they loved sleepovers.

"It's a deal." We sealed it with a kiss.

That night, I wound up sleeping better than I had in years. Every time one of those thoughts that had plagued me for months crawled into my head, I lifted my head from Alex's chest and looked at his face. He made me feel content, confident, and safe in a way no one had before.

We didn't wind up going to the gym the next day. Instead, we all slept in, and then Alex made us pancakes for breakfast.

"These are almost as good as my mom's," Lydia said in between bites.

"What do you think, Jakey?" I asked.

"Yours are better," he said.

Alex made a face, pretending to be wounded, and Jacob laughed.

"We better hurry, guys." I stood to take my dirty plate to the kitchen. "Alex has to leave for work soon."

"You don't have to leave," he said. "As a matter of fact, I was just thinking I should give you a key to my place. That way you guys can come over and use the pool whenever you want."

Jacob and Lydia looked at each other out of the corners of their eyes. Smiles crept across their faces.

"Are you sure about that? There's a pretty big chance we might be over here almost every day." While the kids played in the pool, I could bring my laptop out to the patio and keep an eye on them while I worked. It was actually a genius idea.

"I hate coming home to an empty house. Nothing would make me happier than to hear your kids laughing as I walk up to my door after a long day at work."

I could tell by the tone of his voice how much he missed Leah. I laced my fingers through his. "You'll get her back. I just know it."

"I hope so," Alex replied.

"We won't stop fighting until you do."

"We?"

"That's right. You heard me."

He put his hand on my cheek. "I love you, Vanessa."

"I love you too," I said for the first time. Then I gave him a kiss.

The kids both started giggling and oohing. It had been years since they'd seen me kiss their father, so they weren't really used to public displays of affection, but it was good for them to see what two people loving each other was supposed to look like.

LATER THAT DAY, after the kids and I returned home, I realized that I felt lighter than I had in a long time. Opening up to Alex made it feel like a load had been lifted off my shoulders. Doubts would find a way to creep back inside my head, but the more I thought about it, the more I realized Alex was right. I'd never know what had been going through Ryan's head the morning that he died, but whatever it was, his death wasn't my fault. Ryan had issues that he needed help to deal with. I'd told him as much time and time again, but he never listened. He didn't want to pay a stranger to listen to his problems. Apparently, that's what I was there for. But Ryan's demons were too big for me to slay. And now it was too late. He was dead. The car accident that took his life was a tragic accident. Maybe if Ryan had lived, I could've one day convinced him to go to counseling, and maybe he could've become a better man, but it was too late for that.

I needed to figure out how to breathe again and appreciate that through some crazy stroke of luck, I'd been given a second chance at love.

EPILOGUE

A few weeks later, my turn came to help Alex through a rough patch. Kristi had finally made good on her threat to tell Leah that Alex wasn't her father. Leah called sobbing. The kids and I were at Alex's place enjoying a late dinner. I could hear her tears through the phone. Alex went into the bedroom to talk in private. A few minutes later he returned, his face ashen.

"What happened?" I asked, taking his hand.

"Kristi introduced Leah to her biological dad. Apparently, she's dating him now."

I turned to the kids. "Why don't you two go watch some TV while Alex and I clean up?"

They didn't need to be told twice. TV beat clearing the table any day of the week.

"Is Leah okay?"

"She's furious," he said. "She wants me to drive up to Pollock Pines and pick her up so she doesn't have to be around Kristi and her new boyfriend. When I explained that I couldn't do that, she just cried."

"This must be heartbreaking for you."

He ran his hands over his face. "I want full custody, but I know I'll never get it. I tried to explain that to Leah, but she doesn't understand how these things work."

"Her mother just dropped a bomb on her," I said. "Give her time. She'll calm down."

Alex made a fist. For a moment, I thought he'd punch the wall behind him, but with the kids in the other room, he must've thought better of it.

I was hopeful that Kristi's little stunt would help Alex's chances in court, but his lawyer was less optimistic. She told Alex the best thing he could hope for was joint custody. That unless the courts deemed Kristi unfit, they wouldn't grant Alex full custody.

Family court moved at a snail's pace. The waiting was the hardest part for Alex. Even though he got to see Leah every other weekend, I could tell the stress of not knowing if that would wind up a permanent thing or not got to him.

After weeks and weeks of waiting, his court date finally arrived. Summer was over, and Jacob and Lydia were back in school. Alex and I drove to the courthouse together on a Wednesday morning. He held my hand tightly, clearly anxious. His lawyer had warned him that things could get ugly at these hearings.

As we climbed the courthouse steps, we heard Alex's name being called. He looked over his shoulder. It was Linda, his attorney.

"I've been trying to reach you for the past hour."

"Sorry. I turned my ringer off. Figured it wouldn't look good if my phone went off in the middle of the hearing."

"That's just the thing," Linda said. "There's not going to be a hearing. Your ex-wife's attorney finally convinced her that fighting you in court was a losing battle."

Alex's eyes widened. "You're kidding me, right?"

Linda shook her head. "Nope. Kristi has apparently agreed to joint custody."

"This feels too good to be true," Alex said.

"Trials are expensive, and there's little doubt in my mind that you would have won. Kristi must've finally realized that. Or maybe she kept hoping you'd drop the case and this whole thing would go away, but when she figured out that wasn't going to happen she gave up."

"She played her final card when she told Leah the truth," I said.

Alex dropped my hand and hugged his lawyer first, then me. "Tell me I'm not dreaming," he said.

"You're not dreaming."

"Nope, you're not," Linda said. "I'll be in touch with the final paperwork soon. Congratulations."

Alex let out a loud whoop. "We need to celebrate."

"Oh my God, Alex. I'm so happy for you." I hugged him again. I'd come to think of Leah as family. So did Jacob and Lydia. She had a beautiful, gentle soul just like her dad.

We had to wait a few more days to celebrate. Alex took off work early on Friday afternoon, and we all piled into his car, anxious to get up to Pollock Pines and pick Leah up from her mother's house.

I caught my first glimpse of Kristi when she opened the door for Alex. She was nothing liked I'd pictured her. Her hair was dyed an unnatural shade of blond. She wore workout clothes which revealed a model-perfect body. But I didn't feel even a pang of envy. She was attractive on the outside, but inside was another story entirely.

When we got back to Sacramento, we stopped for pizza. The kids had unanimously agreed that's what they wanted for dinner. Neither Alex nor I were surprised. Pizza seemed to win every time. Since it was a special occasion, I even let the kids get soda.

Alex lifted his glass. "I want to make a toast," he said. "To family."

I smiled. Those two words were perfect. They summed up what our little gathering was all about.

"To family," we repeated before clinking glasses together.

I glanced at everyone's face. There were happy smiles all around. We weren't what anyone would call a traditional family, but that didn't matter. We loved each other. Things wouldn't always be easy, but Alex and I had each other's backs. And blood or not, we were a family.

WANT to be notified when Teresa Roman's next book will be released? Then sign up for her mailing list by going to http://eepurl.com/ddSrh9. Your email address will never be shared, and you can unsubscribe at any time.

Word of mouth and reviews are essential for an author's success. If you enjoyed this book, please consider leaving a review. Even a short review would be helpful and greatly appreciated.

Thank you.

Connect with me online.
Website: www.teresaromanwrites.com
Facebook: www.facebook.com/teresaromanauthor
Twitter: www.twitter.com/TRomanauthor
Goodreads:
www.goodreads.com/author/show/14163515.Teresa_Roman
Instagram: www.instagram.com/teresaromanauthor/

ALSO BY TERESA ROMAN

ACKNOWLEDGMENTS

This was a hard book to write. We're all familiar with stories of domestic violence, but less so with stories of emotional abuse. For anyone who's experienced abuse of any kind, I hope this book helps you realize you aren't alone.

I'd like to thank my children for their patience and support while Mommy spent hours in front of the computer writing. I'd like to thank my sister whose writing advise is priceless. You can't even begin to know how much I appreciate you taking the time from your busy life to read my first messy drafts. I'd also like to thank my editor, Linda Cassidy Lewis, who is not only an editor, but an amazing author (seriously, you should check her books out). I'd like to thank my friend, Rebecca, for her writing advice and for helping me craft the perfect blurb for this book. Last but definitely not least, like always, I want to thank you, my readers. Your support means so much to me.

ABOUT THE AUTHOR

Teresa Roman writes contemporary and paranormal romance for adults and young adults. If it were possible to be born with a book in her hands, that's how Teresa Roman would've entered this world. Her passion for reading is what inspired her to become a writer. She loves the way stories can take you to another time and place.

Born in Romania, Teresa has lived in the Midwest and on both coasts but currently calls Sacramento, California, her home. She lives there with her husband, three adorable children, three cats, and a dog. When she's not at her day job or running around with her kids, you can find her in the kitchen, baking a sinful treat, in front of the computer, writing, or with her head buried in another book.